MYSTERY AT MALABAR COTTAGE

MANJIRI PRABHU

Readomania

Readomania Publishing
A division of Kurious Kind Media Private Limited
908, Vishwadeep Building, District Centre, Janakpuri,
New Delhi – 110058
books.readomania.com
email: contact@readomania.com
Facebook: facebook.com/iamreadomania
Twitter: twitter.com/iamreadomania
Instagram: iamreadomania

First Published in 2019 by Readomania

ISBN: 978-93-85854-82-8

Illustrations by Mistunee Chowdhury

Typeset in Palatino Linotype by Shine Graphics
Printed at Thomson Press (India) Ltd.

Readomania

India has traditionally been the land of storytellers and a lot of us have an inherent skill of creating good plots, good stories and good narrations. With a little encouragement and support, many more authors will be widely read and attain a place in the sun. This is the essence of *Readomania*—an initiative that nurtures emerging stars of the literary world.

It would not be an exaggeration to say that *Readomania* is the talent hunt in fiction. It goes a step beyond by not just identifying the talent but also nurturing it and showcasing it to the world. In the process, we have created a powerhouse of content.

Readomania has four principal interest areas—traditional print publishing, online library of short stories and poetry, literary events and products.

The print publishing works towards delivering good quality content to the readers. We publish good authors in meaningful anthologies, novels and works of narrative non-fiction. Our books stand out for their perspectives, the plots, the language and most importantly their ability to enrich lives.

Take a break, read something nice, write something beautiful. Read our books or visit us at www.readomania.com and enjoy a whole new world of literature.

To

My nephew Yash Prabhu

The Star of the Future…

Malabar Cottage

The children heard the shrill screech of brakes before they saw the car. A green car suddenly appeared from behind and overtook them over a curve at such breakneck speed that Mrs Desai pulled the wheel of her car to the left with a sharp jerk. The children were almost thrown sideways. Within minutes, the dilapidated car had gathered speed and vanished from sight.

'Crazy man!' Mrs Desai exclaimed, furiously. 'He could have killed us!'

'*They* would have killed us. There were two men in the car,' Samir added with an edge of anger to his voice.

'How dare they drive like that on such a narrow, curvy road?' fumed Tina. 'Alpana *kaki*, do you think we ought to file a complaint with the police?'

There was a momentary silence as Mrs Desai considered the matter. Finally, she shook her head. 'No, let's just forget it. They are long gone, no point unnecessarily pursuing issues. And we don't even have a proper description to offer the police. Besides, why spoil a perfectly lovely beginning to your holidays?' She smiled at her niece through the mirror.

'But *this was* a most exciting beginning for our hols,' Fulki said. 'I mean, it does predict something exciting for us, doesn't it?'

'Oh God, haven't you given up on your astrological predictions yet, Fulki?' Paras groaned. 'I thought this was your last year's craze.'

Fulki had an unusual hobby each summer. Last year, it was collecting rusted things and the year before last, it was making flower vases out of old records. The children were well-versed with her changing fancies.

'Craze?' Fulki snorted. 'Predictions are an art, they are magic, they are…' she paused, searching for the right word.

At once, everyone grabbed the chance to stir the conversation away from Fulki's boring hobbies. They began speaking about their holidays and very soon the car incident too was totally forgotten.

'It's such a wonderful day for travelling,' Samir remarked. He was fondly called Sam by everyone.

'Oh! I'm so excited!' Fulki exclaimed, bouncing on the seat. The unruly curls around her plump face bounced along with her as if they had springs attached to them. 'How much more time, Mama?'

Mrs Desai smiled. She manoeuvred the car neatly round a bend and said, 'Be patient, we should be there in fifteen minutes.'

'I'm impatient too.' Samir grinned, displaying a charming dimple in his left cheek. 'What fun to stay in a cottage which is more than two hundred years old. A cottage by the sea!'

'We'll be able to bathe and explore around and do just as we please,' Tina said, enjoying the breeze on her face, her two tiny plaits sticking out at odd angles.

'Is the house old, rambling and huge, Alpana *kaki*?' Paras enquired, pushing his spectacles back along the bridge of his nose.

'Don't do that, Paras,' Tina interrupted, frowning at his spectacles. 'You know it's not a good habit to keep fiddling with your specs.'

'Please, you two—no teaching and preaching.' Samir laughed as Paras scowled deeply.

'It's a dear little cottage, not very huge but big enough to house several guests. Panna uses it like some kind of a makeshift hotel for people who don't mind a little bit of discomfort to be with nature.

As a child I really enjoyed my holidays here. It is a perfect place for children, safe and cosy and some of my friends have sent their kids to Malabar Cottage too. Panna has a hawk's eye on all the guests, so the children are in good care and not entirely unsupervised. Some years ago, your father and I had visited for a short holiday and we really enjoyed the peace and the food. I'm sure you will have a splendid time here,' Mrs Desai assured.

Paras and Tina, who lived in Pune, had come to spend their summer vacations with their cousins Fulki and Samir in Mumbai. But Mr and Mrs Desai had to change plans and go to Goa for some important work. It was the latter's idea that the children spend their holidays at the Malabar Cottage, along the coastline and so here they were, on their way.

'Look, there's the sea!' Samir shouted, pointing to the blue stretch of water, which appeared on their left. The waves lashed on the rocks and the children exclaimed with joy.

Soon the sandy beach came in view and four eager heads peeked out of the windows, to observe the Malabar village—a cluster of houses made of red bricks, stones and thatched roofs. There was even a red stone pavement and the village looked as if it was splashed liberally with shades of red.

'It looks so cute! So fairytale-ish, doesn't it?' Fulki remarked. She was eleven, like Tina, and their brothers were a couple of years older.

'It certainly does,' Samir agreed. 'I say, is that our cottage, on top of that hill?'

'It is,' his mother replied and brought the car to a halt. 'Before we proceed, how about something to drink? Or an ice-cream? There's a good shop here.'

The children did not need any invitation. They were out in a trice, glad to quench their thirst and stretch their legs. They all trooped into the shop which was cool and dark inside. Once their eyes got accustomed to the dark, they stared in amazement at the store. It was tightly crammed from top to bottom with all sorts of things! Packets of food, drinks, games, gift articles, and it even had a yellow phone booth tucked into a corner. And from amidst the clutter, an old, withered woman approached them, beaming from ear to ear.

Mrs Desai checked the mini fridge which was bravely shouldering piles of suitcases and ordered apple juice for all them.

'Ah, you're going to that cottage of mine, aren't you?' the old lady beamed. 'A wonderful place, as old as the sea, but there it stands, strong and unbeaten, on the top of the hill.' She spoke in Marathi.

'If I am not mistaken, Panna is your…,' Mrs Desai began.

'Yes, Panna is my daughter. And I know you, don't I? You had come to Malabar Cottage some years ago.'

'I did and I loved it! But this time, only the kids are staying there.' Mrs Desai smiled.

'It's a wonderful old cottage. Generations of my family have lived there and now Panna lives there. You see, I'm too old to walk up that hill, so I live in the village. But my dear Panna is bravely managing that difficult cottage and caring for her guests,' she replied, her wrinkled face beaming.

Her black eyes suddenly sparkled as she added, 'Well, you go and stay there, and if you are lucky, you may find a passage or two. Secret passages, you know.'

The children pricked up their ears. What was this they were hearing?

'Secret passages! Like in story books? Do you mean to say that there are really secret passages in the cottage?' Fulki asked eagerly, her curls bobbing with excitement.

'You can't be serious,' Paras remarked, disbelievingly.

Mrs Desai smiled as she watched the exchange. She remembered how excited *she* had been when she had visited Malabar Cottage for the first time and she understood their enthusiasm.

'Oh, I am very serious and you will be too when you see them,' the old lady nodded.

'But why would anybody build secret passages in an ordinary cottage?' Samir asked.

'Because it is *not* an ordinary cottage,' Tina said. 'Don't you remember, Alpana *kaki* told us that the cottage was special and old and....'

'That's right,' Panna's mother interrupted them with a twinkle in her eyes. 'There were smugglers in those days, you see. They used to hide their smuggled goods in that cottage. It is full of secret ways and tunnels. You will find many if you know where to look...surely, you will. You come to me one day and I shall tell you the story of Pilot-Eye.' She shook a worn finger and smiled wickedly.

'Wow, this gets more and more exciting!' Samir exclaimed, convinced. 'We'll certainly make it a point to visit you one day.'

'Tell us something more. Mama, can we have another juice? It's lovely to hear her talk but its so hot too,' Fulki pleaded.

As Mrs Desai consented, the old lady fetched some more drinks. The sun was hot outside and they were getting late. But Mrs Desai did not have the heart to rush them. She had plenty of time actually, to drop the children off at their destination and return to Mumbai.

'Panna knows many of them,' the lady continued, juggling a few articles in tight spaces. 'She would run all around the house as a child but she was a tremendous help to me. And now look at her, managing that place during the summer and keeping up a good reputation for the cottage.'

They chatted along for a while enjoying the old lady's ramblings and the juice. Samir also took a survey of the store, keeping a sharp lookout for anything unusual to eat.

'Find anything good?' Tina teased.

'Not yet. But such places always have a variety of Konkan spices,' Samir replied.

'It's amazing how you are so fond of cooking, Sam.' Mrs Desai smiled fondly at her son.

'The best part is that we love his concoctions, don't we?' Paras glanced at his siblings and they all nodded.

Samir looked pleased.

Finally, it was time to leave, so the children bid goodbye to the old storekeeper. Mrs Desai hustled them into the car and they were once more on the move.

Soon, the car was crawling up the hill. A few minutes later, Mrs Desai turned into a sandy road which led straight up to the cottage. A sturdy-looking house of rock and brick, with a chimney sticking out of the thatched black roof, slowly came in view. A small garden with tall coconut and mango trees gave the house a quaint look.

The car had barely stopped when the doors were flung open and the children clambered out. They ran to the edge of the cliff and peered down. The sea lashed on the rocks far below them and the view was breathtakingly beautiful.

'Look, we are almost on top of the sea!' Fulki exclaimed, holding her breath and her curls against the onslaught of the strong wind. The sea was like a vast, unending blue-green carpet below them, gleaming and glittering in the sun.

Just then the cottage door swung open and a plump woman walked out, smiling broadly. Brown as bread and draped in a pink cotton sari, she looked like a chocolate cake with lovely icing.

'Ah, here you are at last.' Panna beamed, looking exactly like her mother. 'Come along in, it is cooler inside.'

The four children liked her at once. As she led them into a medium-sized hall with a high ceiling, she talked endlessly with Mrs Desai. They both seemed very pleased to meet each other.

The hall was simply furnished with hand-woven rugs on the stone floor, a sofa in which the children thought they would vanish and a long wall lined with books.

'Wow, just look at those books!' Paras exclaimed, spontaneously pushing his glasses back and totally missing his sister's frown. He adored books and wrote stories too. He planned to be a great writer one day. 'How do we reach the top, Mrs Panna?'

'No one has ever called me that, child.' Panna laughed. 'Just call me Panna and I'll feel a lot younger.'

'Right, Panna.' Paras grinned.

'There's a ladder in the kitchen and you can fetch it whenever you like. Those books are ages old. My family was fond of reading and collected all these books.' She shrugged. 'And now look at them, sitting on top of the shelves and no one has even touched some of them in years. I have such a task keeping them dust-free. But you go ahead and enjoy them—I shall be glad if they are of use to someone.

But what am I doing, standing and chatting with you? The tea is getting cold. Come along and have it first, you must be hungry after the long drive.'

The other five needed no coaxing and followed Panna into the next room. The table was laid with aloo parathas, chutney and home-made, hot samosas.

'I'm going to enjoy myself here,' Samir declared, as they tucked into the delicious spread. 'These parathas are exceptional.'

'You're a wonderful cook, Panna, and you haven't lost your touch.' Mrs Desai smiled. 'I'm glad I brought the children here. It was good of you to have them at the last minute, when you may already have a few guests.'

'Oh, it's no trouble at all. I told you, at the moment, there is only one Mr Jain who keeps to himself and is barely at home. And there are two more people coming over in a couple of days. But don't you worry, the children will remember this Malabar Cottage holiday,' Panna prophesied, grandly.

'I know you will keep an eye on them.' Mrs Desai smiled fondly at the four flushed faces, devouring the tea and snacks. 'And now I must take your leave. There's a lot of packing to be done and I'd like to reach Mumbai before nightfall. Goodbye dear children, enjoy yourselves. Remember, don't go out on the beach at high tide and please, don't be too much of a trouble to Panna.'

'Don't worry about them, I've handled children before and I have a boy of my own, who is the naughtiest in the world, and who also owns the world's "worst dog",' grinned Panna. 'These children will have plenty to see and explore and to keep them busy.'

'Goodbye then and if you think you urgently need to call me...Sam, you have the mobile number, don't you?'

'Yes, Mama.' Samir obediently brandished his small pocketbook.

After removing their luggage from the car boot, the children kissed Mrs Desai goodbye. As the car sped down the hill, they waved to her until she was out of sight.

'Now begin our real holidays.' Fulki sighed happily, as they returned to the cottage.

'And we are going to enjoy them,' Samir added, cheerfully.

'That you will,' Panna nodded. 'Now, come along and I will show you your rooms.' She led them up a small staircase to rooms lined one after the other on either side of the corridor. She opened two of the rooms in the centre.

'This one is for the girls and the other one for the boys. Now better start unpacking and after you finish, you can come down to the kitchen and I shall introduce you to my boy.'

'Right, thanks for everything, Panna,' Paras said.

'That's okay. What would you like for dinner?'

'Dinner! I'm so stuffed that I can't think of food at all!' Tina exclaimed.

'I'm talking about *dinner,* child. And if I know kids at all, by that time you four will be ravenous.' Panna laughed. 'But of course, if you really feel you won't be able to manage a big meal, I can cook up something light for you. Would that be fine?'

'I think so,' Samir agreed and the others gave their consent. 'If you like, I can come help cook.'

Panna stared at him. '*You* will help me cook?' she confirmed.

'Oh, I love cooking!'

Panna laughed. 'Good for you. Maybe you can put some sense into my boy, who hates anything to do with the kitchen except eating. But thanks. I can manage.'

As soon as Panna left them to unpack, Fulki and Tina turned their attention to the room. Though it was sparsely furnished, with a closet and a dressing table, the two beds by the window looked warm and comfortable. A rough hand-woven rug covered the cold stone floor. They looked out of the window and gasped at the view. Miles and miles of water stretched before them, the waves tumbling gently over each other.

'Look! We can see the cove too. This seems to be the deserted part of the beach, doesn't it?' Fulki pointed to the small inlet below them.

'Yes, we can have so much fun! We can even go boating,' Tina replied, smiling happily at the thought. Her oddly angled, stiff plaits made her look funny. 'I would love to try my hand at rowing. I think I'm quite capable of it.'

'So am I,' Fulki added, glancing at her plump form in the mirror. 'You see, I am not all fat, I have plenty of stamina in me.' She grinned good-naturedly, flexing her muscles.

'I don't doubt it,' her cousin laughed.

'Hey, I hope that these holidays and all this outdoor activity will help me reduce a bit. I would love to go back to school, looking trim and slim.' Fulki sighed, yearningly.

'Oh come on, Fulki, being plump suits you, you know.' Tina hugged her. 'All these ample curls would simply lose their charm if you lost weight.'

Fulki laughed. 'Thanks. It makes me feel better.'

'I say, what's that far off? Can you see it?'

Fulki strained her eyes. She could see a hazy form like an island almost in the middle of the sea and a tall, building-like structure rising from it.

'It looks like a building to me, probably a ruin. No doubt we shall explore it. Now hurry up and unpack. I'm glad we've got plenty of rough clothes, Bermuda shorts and swim suits. I can't wait to splash in the water.'

The two of them hastily unpacked their clothes, hanging them neatly in the cupboard and pushing their bags under the bed.

'I wonder if Sam and Paras have finished unpacking yet,' Tina said, opening the door and peeping down the corridor.

A tall man was moving down the passage, frowning and checking his pockets. He was lean, his thin cheeks covered with stubble and he wore a pair of blue jeans and a white T-shirt. He stopped and continued to check his pockets. Suddenly, he looked up and caught Tina staring curiously at him.

A scowl flashed on his face. 'Who are you?' he asked, bluntly.

'I'm Tina,' she replied, a little taken aback with his rude tone.

'Yes, but what are you doing here?' he persisted, in the same irritated voice.

'We've come to spend our holidays here,' Tina answered, getting a little annoyed.

'We? You mean there are more of you?'

He sounded as if they were a different kind of species.

'Yes, we are four of us and we plan to stay here for a month,' Fulki replied. She had just stepped out of her room and had overheard the exchange.

'I don't believe it,' the man muttered. 'I was clearly told that there would be no kids here. I must talk to Panna.' With that he stalked off down the corridor.

'Who was that?' Fulki whispered.

'I think, it must be that Mr Jain, Panna was telling us about. He sure does not look a friendly sort,' Tina remarked.

'If he hadn't had that rude tone as if we were trespassing on his property, I would have almost predicted him to be good-looking.'

'You don't need to predict that, he is sort of handsome.' Tina claimed to be an authority on looks.

The boys came out of their room just then and the girls told them what had transpired.

'Well, he can jolly well keep out of our way if he doesn't like us.' Paras pushed back his specs indignantly. 'Anyway, let's not spoil our evening. We can go down to the beach and relax in the sand.'

'And we've also made a discovery. We've just realised that the high tide will come in soon, so we won't be able to explore the deserted part of the beach today,' Samir announced.

'Next time then, we must remember as we possibly cannot disobey *Kaki*. She particularly warned us about high tides,' Tina agreed.

The four of them went down to the kitchen, chatting continuously. High tides and rude neighbours did not dampen their spirits. They had made up their minds to have fun and they had plenty of time to explore everything. One whole month! And that was a great deal for four children who were determined to enjoy themselves at all cost.

Fulki's Crystal Ball

A dog began barking loudly just as the Desai children entered the kitchen. They stopped short, surprised.

'Ruffy! Stop barking!' a small boy shouted. He was about nine, dressed in khaki shorts. He was holding the collar of a ferocious-looking dog, who continued to growl menacingly.

Fulki retreated behind her brother, for she was very scared of dogs.

'What is your prediction about this dog, Fulki?' Samir asked with laughter in his voice and his sister made a face at him. Panna smiled reassuringly.

'You needn't be afraid, Fulki. Ruffy is as harmless as a butterfly. This is just his way of greeting you, for the first time. He's trying to show off! Now stop that barking, Ruffy,' she addressed the dog sternly. 'They are friends, *friends*...understand? Come on, now. Shake hands like a good boy. They are our guests. Come on!'

The black Pomeranian certainly seemed to understand, for he cocked his head on one side, listening intently to Panna and then turning to the small boy expectantly. He appeared to be very loyal to his little master.

The boy smiled shyly at the children and patted Ruffy. 'Shake hands, Ruffy, old boy.'

Much to the children's amazement, the dog obediently put up his right paw, his tongue hanging out. Samir moved forward cautiously and held the outstretched paw. Then very slowly, his other hand patted Ruffy's big head.

'Good boy, Ruffy! How are you?'

One by one the children shook hands cautiously, Fulki being the last one. Panna and the others urged her, as she flatly refused to approach the dog at first. But as she lightly held the paw, keeping a safe distance between them, Ruffy suddenly licked her hand. She was so surprised that she started laughing.

'Ruffy likes you and he's telling you not to be afraid of him,' the small boy interpreted, solemnly.

'I hope so,' Fulki remarked doubtfully, retreating into a corner quickly.

But Ruffy really seemed to have taken a fancy to her. He began sniffing her toes and legs and Fulki squealed. 'Oh, please call him off, he's tickling me!' she cried, as the cold nose touched her feet.

'Just stand still, he won't hurt you,' Paras advised.

Fulki did so, watching Ruffy with large, frightened eyes. Finally, the dog treated her with another lavish lick and she ventured a brief pat on his back.

'Okay Ruffy, please go now, please,' she begged.

The others laughed as Ruffy obediently sat down in a corner.

'He's a good dog though quite naughty,' Panna explained. 'Well, this is my son Vijju. He will show you around if you wish. But of course, I wouldn't like him to interfere in any of your plans. But if you need him, he will gladly accompany you.' She introduced the children one by one to Vijju, who was initially a little shy, but gradually opened up.

'Are there caves around here?' Samir wanted to know.

'Oh yes, quite a lot of them. And there are some, which I alone have discovered and not another soul is aware of them,' Vijju replied, proudly.

'Great! Will you show them to us?' Paras asked, peering at him from behind his specs.

'Of course,' Vijju nodded, readily.

'And what about secret passages? Are there any in this cottage?' Tina asked curiously. 'Panna, your mother said there were tons of them in this house, that in the olden days, smugglers used them to carry loot.'

'Yes, that's right, but Vijju will be your guide in these matters. He knows every nook and cranny like he was the architect of this cottage. I used to run in and out of these tunnels, once upon a time, but that seems almost like a lifetime ago and I don't even remember most of them now. Why, I haven't been in one for several years now!' She grinned.

'Years! When you are in the midst of loads of secret passages?' Fulki exclaimed.

It certainly sounded odd. They all loved anything exciting and adventurous. How could Panna stay with secret passages under her nose and not be in one for years?

'I would have gone crazy if I were you,' Samir remarked, honestly and Panna laughed at the idea.

'Not if you were in my shoes. I have gone through these passages over a thousand times. I had been as excited as you four when I was a kid, but too much of anything kind of takes the charm away. I got so used to these hidden passages that I have got over them. Though, I wouldn't mind an occasional peep to revive old memories.' She winked, then turned to busy herself with her cooking. 'Now, go to the beach and don't waste any more time chatting with me. Vijju, show them around and take Ruffy along with you. He's been eyeing the chicken for some time and I don't want to risk having him in the kitchen. The moment my back is turned, poof, the chicken will be in his stomach!'

Ruffy looked at them as if he was grinning. He knew when someone was talking about him. The children began liking him a little and even Fulki admitted that he did not look as fierce as he appeared at first sight.

'Come on, Ruffy, out of the room,' Vijju ordered and the dog obeyed meekly.

The five of them, along with their furry friend, walked down the hill in the evening sun. A cool wind had picked up, playing with their hair and T-shirts. It was when they were crossing over to the beach that Samir suddenly stopped.

'Look, isn't that the same car, which almost pushed us off the road?' He pointed to a dilapidated green car parked in front of a store.

'It sure looks like the same one,' Tina agreed.

'I have a good mind to hang around and give whoever is driving a piece of my mind!' Samir remarked, angrily. But there was no one around.

'Do you know if this car belongs to anyone around here, Vijju?' Paras asked.

'I've never seen it before.' Vijju shrugged.

'I wonder who it belongs to and what it is doing here,' Tina said, as they made their way to the beach.

A few children were playing and running around, as their parents relaxed on the sand. The Desai children chose a nice spot where they could stretch and watch the golden sun sinking over the horizon and feel the blue-green water swishing towards them. The island, with the ruined building was quite clearly visible now.

'That's Malabar Island...,' Vijju explained, '... with the old, ruined castle. Rumour has it that in those days, if the smugglers caught anyone spying on them, they would hold them captive by taking them over to the island and leaving them in the dungeons of the castle to perish and die.' He spoke quietly and with a bit of reverence in his voice.

'What an awful thing to do!' Fulki exclaimed, appalled at the idea.

'Who told you all this?' Samir asked, curiously.

'My *Ajji* (grandmother). She tells me hundreds of stories, some of which she actually witnessed herself. She even told me that the prisoners were never taken across to the island by boat. Because nobody ever saw them!'

'But if they were not transported by boat, how were they taken? Is there another way to reach the island?' Tina asked. She was lying on her back, her arms cushioning her head and blinking at the sun.

Vijju looked thoughtful for a minute. 'We have worked this out, over and over again—*Ajji* and me. *Ajji* told me that there is an underground tunnel, which runs from the mainland to the island. Of course, no one has ever discovered it. It was a big secret and it died with the smugglers. And if anyone has discovered it, they never revealed it. I have searched most of the caves, because the tunnel—if one exists—is well hidden. As yet, I have found nothing, but I don't intend to give up. I shall find it one day,' the small boy spoke in a low determined voice.

The other four experienced a thrill of excitement. An underground tunnel that runs below the sea! What could be more wonderful? This was something they had only read about in storybooks. Would they be able to find the tunnel? What fun to search high and low, going through caves, to uncover the possibly long-lost tunnel!

'May we help you look for it?' Paras asked.

Vijju hesitated a second, then grinned. 'I guess there's no harm. In fact, the more the merrier. *Aai* (mother) once said that it was probably in the deserted cove. Boats would come in late at night into the cove and my great-grandma would often lie awake at night and peep through the window to watch the bobbing lights.'

'The prisoners were taken in the dead of night then?' Samir asked.

Everyone sat still, listening intently.

Vijju shrugged. 'No one knew when and how they were carried to and fro, to the island. What great-grandma saw was the unloading of the smuggled goods. She was such a kid then, she did not follow half the things she saw. Her father was one of the partners and every night when the all-safe signal was given, a rowing boat would land in the cove. The cargo would be removed and hidden in one of the secret rooms of the cottage. After a few days, when everything seemed clear, the goods were sent to their respective places.'

The cousins were silent. It was all very fascinating—the boat lapping at the cove, in the middle of the night, the hushed, low voices, the scraping of trunks and goods—it all sounded most interesting.

'Goodness! I shouldn't have told you about the smuggler in the family. *Ajji* will be most upset!' Vijju looked alarmed.

'Don't be silly,' Tina spoke up, patronisingly. 'This was all a long time ago and no one will bother anymore. But it does sound rather thrilling, doesn't it?'

'It does. I almost wish I was born in those times,' Paras said, wistfully. 'I would rather become a smuggler and lead an adventurous life than study boring lessons at school.'

'Well, for all you know you may have been one in your last life!' Fulki remarked, airily. 'After all....'

'No, please! Spare me your knowledge of science and astrology,' Paras cut her short and Fulki frowned.

'Don't make fun of me,' she said, darkly. 'My predictions are accurate, you wait and watch. This crystal of mine is most fascinating...' She extracted a small crystal ball from her pocket and the others pounced on her again.

'You still have that bit of glass that gypsy gave you last hols?' Samir exclaimed.

'Yes, and it tells me a lot of things,' she replied, with a toss of her ample curls.

'Would it tell me if I can become a chef when I grow up?' he taunted.

'You don't need a crystal ball to predict *that*,' Fulki scoffed.

Vijju looked most interested. 'Can you really tell the future?' he asked, curiously.

The others groaned, as Fulki turned to him with an important expression on her plump face. 'Yes, and if you people would care to listen, I can tell you what is going to happen these hols.'

'Okay, shoot. Tell us once and for all.' Tina spoke in a resigned tone.

Samir stifled a laugh, as his sister stared deep into the crystal for a moment. Her voice changed into a deep and resonant rumble as she said, 'I can foresee a lot of excitement, plenty of fun and yes... we are going to find the tunnel. And we also have to be careful—I can see water and even guns!' she ended on a high dramatic note and except for Vijju, everyone smiled.

He stared at her in wonder. 'Wow, if all that comes true, I'll ask you to read my future again.'

'Thank you. My predictions *always* come true.' Fulki tucked the crystal back into her pocket, calmly ignoring the wink Paras flashed his cousins.

Ruffy got up, feeling bored with inactivity. He seemed to be quite at ease with the children now. The dog stood wagging his fluffy tail and began digging a hole in the sand with all his paws. Sand flew all over their faces.

'Hey Ruffy! Stop that, we don't want to be buried alive!' Samir exclaimed, dusting himself and laughing.

But Ruffy had other ideas. He continued his digging with a fresh bout of energy, till all the children stood up indignantly. Then barking joyously, he ran round them, jumping and snapping playfully at their ankles.

Vijju laughed. 'He wants to play with you. You have to run in different directions and he will chase you. Do you mind playing?'

'Of course not!' the others chorused.

Soon all five of them were racing on the beach, hair and sand flying. Ruffy was thrilled and he raced after each one of them, woofing joyously and wagging his tail like a flapping sail in the wind. The children were breathless when they finally stopped but their faces glowed with happiness. They had thoroughly enjoyed their evening and there was more to come.

'You are a wonderful dog, Ruffy—the best in the world!' Tina thumped Ruffy fondly on the back.

He, at once, returned her affection with a large wet lick of his own. He agreed with her!

As they chatted and started walking back to the cottage, they noticed that the green car was still in position. They were just about to pass it, when two men appeared from the store, carrying a big mattress between them.

Samir alerted the others with a raised hand and they stopped.

'You are not going to go and talk to them, Sam,' Tina hissed. 'Forget them!'

'Oh, don't worry. I am just curious about them,' Samir assured her but he was staring hard at the two strangers.

One was tall with a rather unkempt, long beard. He wore a scarf round his neck and chewed a paan with red liquid dribbling down from the side of his mouth. He was clad in an expensive-looking red silk kurta with a matching lungi. He was rasping orders at the other fellow, who was a man of medium height with a shining bald head. There was a sullen expression on his face, as he obeyed the instructions.

'Come on, we've seen enough. Why do you want to bother yourself with some irresponsible strangers we shall never meet again?' Paras tugged at his cousin's arm.

Samir shrugged and they turned toward the hill. 'They sure did look like an odd pair. I'm sure the one in the kurta was driving the car. He had that smug, overconfident stance that I truly dislike.'

'Forget them. God, I'm so awfully hungry, whatever will Panna say?'

But Panna, knowing children, had a splendid meal of fish curry and fried *halwa* fish ready for them. Samir asked her so many questions on the preparation, that she was delighted and patiently responded to his eager curiosity. She even promised to give him her 'secret recipes' and Samir was pleased.

That night the Desai children retired to bed early. They had had a tiring day and they wanted to start exploring early and fresh the next morning.

Tina stood by the window for a while, observing the dark shape of the island far away, and thinking of all that Vijju had told them. It was an awful thing to do—leaving people in the dungeons to perish—hard to believe, but it must be true. And the underground tunnel? Well, if there was one and if Fulki's predictions came true, they would definitely find it. She yawned. Fulki was already in bed, so Tina slipped beneath the warm covers. The cool, salty breeze swept into the room and as her drowsy eyelids drooped slowly, she knew that they were going to enjoy themselves tremendously.

The First Secret Room

The early morning sun streamed in through the open window, waking up the boys. Samir jumped out of bed energetically and went to wash up in the tiny sink. The tap water was cold and he splashed it on his face. He pulled the sheets off Paras, almost dragging him to the floor.

'Hey! I'm getting up,' Paras protested, laughing.

Within minutes they were dressed and knocking on the next door. Their cousins were ready, much to their surprise. Soon they were all walking on the cliff, peering out at the beautiful orange landscape.

'Isn't it heavenly?' Tina breathed in the morning freshness with deep satisfaction.

'Invigorating,' Paras agreed, warming up with some bending exercises.

'I'm going to meditate for a while,' Fulki declared.

'Don't you think you're overdoing this a little bit, Fulki?' Samir asked with a frown.

'No, I'm as serious about this as you are about... about whatever it is that you are serious about... Yes, your cooking,' she said in a grave tone and the others gave up in exasperation. Fulki sometimes took herself too seriously.

She chose a flat stone facing the endless glittering, dark sea, sat cross-legged and closed her eyes.

Paras shrugged. 'Maybe she *knows* what she's doing.' He smiled. He was very fond of his cousin and ready to make excuses for her odd and sometimes adult-like behaviour.

The others chatted, strolling along the cliff edge and admiring the peach-pink sky, slowing changing to bright crimson.

'Look who's approaching, it's Mr Jain,' Tina said and the others looked in the direction she was staring.

Attired in a black, close-fitting track suit, Jain was jogging up the hill, looking fit and in form. He had an athletic built and Tina wondered why she had earlier thought that he was thin. He jogged right up to the cliff, ignoring the children as if they did not exist and cooled down with some easy exercises. As he swung his arms around and bent down, Tina noticed a small bulge in his back pocket. It was round and small like an elongated ball. What could it be? Something about the shape seemed familiar. And then as she stared, rather shamelessly at the man's bent backside, that *something* edged upwards, revealing the top. It was black and gleaming. Tina's jaw dropped, but she shut it immediately because just at that moment, the man turned and looked straight at her. His gaze was dark and penetrating and Tina hastily looked away. Without a word, Jain sauntered away and entered the cottage.

Tina realised that she was holding her breath. 'Whew, I've made a most important discovery just now!' she exclaimed. 'Did you boys notice anything in that man's back pocket?'

Her cousins shook their heads.

'I'll never make fun of Fulki again.' She expelled a low breath.

'What do you mean?' Paras asked, pushing back his glasses but his sister was too absorbed to stop him.

'A small gun... There was a small gun in his pocket!'

'What!' the boys chorused.

Fulki joined them just then and Tina repeated what she said. Instead of looking triumphant, Fulki appeared stunned.

'Are you sure?' she asked, wide-eyed.

'Positive. I didn't see the gun—I mean the whole of it, but I saw the top protruding and I've seen too many films to not recognise a pistol when I see it.'

'But what is Jain doing with a pistol?' Samir wondered.

'And, more important, what makes him carry it even when he is exercising?' Paras added.

The children looked at each other, suddenly aware that perhaps they had stumbled onto something unsettling. They were quiet for a minute, each of them thinking about the startling discovery.

'Let's not speak about this to anyone. It may just be possible that the man fears someone or something and carries the pistol for his own safety,' Samir said.

'Okay, but I am curious. I want to know more,' Tina stated flatly. 'It wouldn't do any harm, would it, if we just made some casual enquiries with Panna, about the man's whereabouts, background and so on.'

'It wouldn't,' Paras grinned. 'And I'm with you. I want to know more too.'

'Good. Come on, let's go in for breakfast,' Samir remarked, cheerfully.

The four children trooped into the dining room, where Panna was busy laying out the plates and a delicious spread of cream cakes, chocolate biscuits and hot *upma*. The children were so hungry that they forgot their mission, as they tucked in.

'We are going to have two more guests tomorrow. Sagar*ji* is a great scientist and he often likes to work here. He finds it very inspiring—that's what he told me the last time he was here. Of course, you children will have to keep out of his way and make as little noise as possible in the house. He's a brilliant man but ill-tempered. So, it's best to keep away.'

'Don't worry, we shan't bother anyone,' Samir promised.

'I seem to have heard that name before,' Tina was thoughtful. 'Oh yes! He's the scientist who turned up with a project worth several crores. Is he the same person?'

The others looked at Tina with respect. She was so well-informed, reading the newspaper regularly. Unlike Paras who drifted into his world of imagination from time to time, his sister took pains to keep in touch with reality.

'That's right. And the government accepted it and offered him a job, which he refused,' Panna replied, proudly. 'He is on another project now, more important. He barely leaves his room, when he is working, which is fortunate because Ruffy can be such a nuisance with old people. Once he actually managed to slip into Sagar*ji*'s room and chewed up two of his papers! Fortunately, they were trash, but Sagar*ji* was livid. That is why I never trust Ruffy.'

'Oh *Aai*!' Vijju protested. 'He isn't as bad as you make him out to be. Sagar*ji* left his door open, and how was Ruffy to know that he is not supposed to enter the room?' Vijju defended his pet and his mother shook her head in mock anger.

The children glanced at the subject of discussion. Ruffy was sitting quietly beside his master, silently devouring the titbits that were being dropped his way. He looked big, safe and harmless. Certainly not the naughty, mischief-maker he was being labelled as!

'And then there's Mrs Fernando, holidaying with us for the first time. I believe she is some kind of a writer—she may arrive shortly too,' Panna began clearing the dishes.

'And there's a Mr Jain here, already, isn't it? I met him yesterday in the corridor and he didn't seem too happy to know that we were here,' Tina said, innocently.

'Oh yes, he did come and ask me what you kids were doing here. You see, I had told him earlier that there wouldn't be any, but that did not include emergencies. I could never turn your mother down, could I? I explained to him and he accepted.'

'What does he do? I mean is he on a holiday too?' Samir asked, too casually.

'Oh, I believe he is some kind of a businessman. He had been unwell for a while and now he is here convalescing. He is hoping that the sea air will help him recover faster. Now, if you children have finished, you can help me clear the table.'

The four glanced at each other—convalescing! He looked as fit as any one of them. And where did the pistol fit in? But they couldn't discuss it before Panna and hastily finished their breakfast.

Soon Vijju and a prancing Ruffy were leading them down a sandy path, behind the cottage. It was rocky and a little slippery and the children were glad they had worn good, comfortable shoes. But Vijju ran on ahead, sure-footed and nimble, and Samir watched him enviously. What a funny boy he was, sometimes as quiet as a mouse and sometimes active and forthcoming. Perhaps living amidst caves and secret passages with Ruffy as company, made him like that.

'Can we hire boats here?' Fulki asked, as they climbed down the cliff.

'You have to go down to the next village for that. But if you want to go boating, I can lend you mine. I have my own little boat,' Vijju beamed. 'I keep it in the cove and sometimes, when *Aai* wants me out of the way, I row across to the island.'

'Wow! You're lucky,' Samir smiled. 'Is it big enough to accommodate all of us?'

'I think so. Baba gave it to me last summer for my birthday. It's a beauty! I'm sure you will like it.'

They ran down the last bit of the path and arrived at the cove. It was bigger than they had imagined. A huge rock hung over a small inlet of blue water, covering the beach like a natural shelter. The water swept over the smooth, sandy floor and the tiny rocks. It was a lovely place, cool and tranquil.

'I keep my boat here,' Vijju pointed to an opening in the cliff, inside the hanging rock. It was dark inside but the small boy waded in unhesitatingly and Ruffy splashed in after him.

'Bend your head and follow,' Vijju's voice was muffled.

The children waded through the opening and found themselves in another tiny cove. A part of the cliff had caved in, creating space and enclosing it with jutting rocks which looked dangerously like jagged knives. And tied firmly to these rocks was a medium-size red boat, bobbing gently in the ankle-deep water.

'Isn't it a beauty?' Vijju asked, touching the boat reverently.

'Yes, it's great! And I'm sure it will hold all of us,' Paras remarked.

'Yes, we'll just about manage to squeeze in. Do you like the colour? I painted it myself. Baba suggested it. He said, it would look charming and bright with a bit of colour,' the proud owner explained.

'Where is your father now?' Fulki asked, as they waded back into the outer cove.

'He does farming in the countryside, but he comes here often.'

The children sat down on the beach and took off their socks and shoes. The sun was hot and they would dry fast. Then they plunged into the water and splashed around, enjoying the warm water, taking care not to go too far out into the sea. Chatting like babblers, they soon came out of the water, dried themselves, then followed Ruffy and his master again. They were going to see the caves now!

True to his word, Vijju took them through some dark gaping holes, in the cliff-side. What seemed like shallow openings at first turned out to be caves of different shapes and sizes and the children thoroughly enjoyed themselves, exploring in the light of Vijju's torch. The single torchlight illuminated and cut a way through the cave, as their feet shuffled on the sandy floor. All of a sudden the small tunnel, opened into a big room. The children gathered inside, with Ruffy pushing against their legs.

'Barrels!' Samir exclaimed. The light beam had caught the several barrels lying in a corner.

'I think wine used to be brought in those days. The barrels smell of nothing but mustiness now, so we can never know. But *Ajji* says it was wine,' Vijju's voice sounded strange in the small room.

It was damp and cold in the confined space and Fulki shivered. It wouldn't be very thrilling to come here in the dead of night, without a torch. Rather a frightening prospect, she thought. She was quite glad, when they retraced their steps. Ruffy did not like the room either, because he gave a little whine and ran on ahead, his feet pattering softly on the sandy carpet.

The warm sunshine was pleasant after the damp and the dark. 'Much as I like to explore these long-lost caves, I prefer the natural, pure sunshine,' Fulki announced, breathing in the salty air.

'I agree with you.' Paras grinned.

Since it was lunch time, the children trudged back, their appetites whetted with all the tramping on the cliff. They soundly enjoyed the enormous lunch of prawns, rice and *solkadi.* Ruffy went round the table unashamed, waiting patiently for the generous pieces that were being dropped for him.

'He's getting totally pampered and putting on so much weight,' Panna warned as a contented Ruffy returned to his corner for his own food. 'Vijju, you better exercise him a bit. I certainly don't want a fat and lazy dog on my hands.'

The others laughed. Ruffy was certainly beginning to look plump, like a round ball of soft, black fur. Fulki guiltily glanced at herself. Well, *she* had better be careful too! She didn't want to return to school looking healthier than before.

Once lunch was over, the five of them lazed around in the sitting room, doing nothing in particular. The huge meal made them drowsy and one by one they dozed off on the carpet. Minutes later when Panna peeped in to see what they were doing, they were all fast asleep, with Ruffy keeping one eye open for emergencies. She smiled in amusement and went back to her work.

Paras was the first one to wake up and roused the others.

'Oh no! How did we fall asleep? I would rather have explored the secret passages,' Samir groaned.

'We still can,' Tina reminded.

'Vijju, do you feel up to showing us something?' Fulki asked, stifling a yawn.

All of them were awake by now. Vijju gave a loud yawn and grinned. He looked cute with his tousled crop of hair. 'Okay, but we need the torch again. I'll fetch it in a moment.'

He returned in a trice. 'Now, look at this wood-panelled wall. It's not only for decoration, there's something in here. Can you find it?' he asked importantly but with a twinkle in the eye.

The wall was bare except for a lamp which was firmly fixed in a corner. It would be easy to tap and find any hollow panels. So, they set about tapping with their knuckles. A few panels did sound hollow but try as they did, they could find no opening. Vijju watched with a satisfied gleam in his eyes, as the others pushed and pressed in vain. Ruffy, thinking that this was some kind of game, joined them, sniffing and getting under their feet.

'Well, I give up,' Paras was the first to speak. 'My knuckles are all sore with the tapping!'

'Same here. Come on, Vijju. Don't stand there grinning triumphantly, I'm really curious to know what it is and where it is,' Tina suggested.

'I'll show you in a jiffy,' Vijju replied, chuckling. 'Make way everybody.'

He moved to the lamp and said, 'Watch!'

To the children's great surprise, the boy slowly turned the glass lamp to his right. Simultaneously, two panels glided noiselessly, leaving a square gap in the wall.

The children stared in amazement.

'What a trick! I would have never imagined it to work like that!' Fulki exclaimed, as they crowded towards the hole.

'How does it work? Is there a gadget connected to the lamp?' Samir asked, his technical mind very curious.

'I haven't a clue,' Vijju replied. 'But I suppose you are right. It is a small room, too small to accommodate all of us. But you can go in one by one.'

'I was waiting for the invitation.' Tina laughed. 'Come on, Paras. Get in first.'

One by one they crowded into the empty space. There was barely room to stand straight. Samir took the torch Vijju handed to him and shone it around. There was a small stool in a corner with an oil lamp on it, otherwise the room was rough stone walls and floor.

'Are these your things? I mean the stool and lamp?' Fulki asked.

'Yes, I sit and read occasionally, when there are no guests at the cottage. It feels so adventurous and cosy, doesn't it?'

The others agreed heartily. It was most exciting to actually be standing in a secret room that was more than a hundred years old. The air was closed and stuffy but a sense of adventure did hang in the air. Everyone wondered what this room could have been used for.

'Perhaps an emergency storeroom? Or it was meant to be just that—a secret room, to hide something or someone?' Samir said, as they climbed out.

'A room for meditation,' Fulki suggested.

'Hmm... Not a bad thought,' Tina responded and the others, for a change did not make fun of her.

'Something is not right, are you all actually agreeing with me without teasing me?' Fulki asked with a grin.

'Of course, we are actually amazed with your predictions about the gun. How did you do it?' Paras laughed.

'I thought as much, you guys finally believe in my predictions. But I won't tell you how I do it. It's my secret! Just let me know when you need some more visions from me.' Fulki grinned.

Vijju closed the panel again, by turning the lamp in the opposite direction and the wooden panel glided smoothly into place. There wasn't the slightest indication or sign to reveal the secret room behind it.

'It is so neatly hidden. The people in those days must be so clever and intelligent to build such rooms.' Samir's voice held admiration. 'When I build a house, I'll make sure there are at least two such rooms in it.'

'Why don't we go back and make a tunnel from our garden to the ground opposite the street? Won't it be fun?' Tina laughed.

'Actually, I can show you another passage that runs down to the beach,' Vijju offered.

'All the way to the beach!' they exclaimed together and immediately followed him up the stairs.

Ruffy looked at them with a bored expression. What were these children up to, running in and out of dark holes? Why couldn't they have a nice long walk instead? But nevertheless, he pattered noisily after them.

Vijju led them to the girls' room. Much to their surprise, he rolled back a corner of their rug and revealed a square trap door!

'Right under our noses!' Fulki shouted, as the small boy lifted the trap door.

They all crowded together to peer over the dark hole. Even though the bright torch light pierced through the darkness, they could see nothing but blackness.

'There are some steps, cut in the stone, which lead downwards almost all the way. But they stop a little above the high tide mark. A rope is attached and you have to slide down from there.'

Samir glanced at his watch. 'Oh no! It's past six. No chance of exploring the passage today. The tide must be well in,' he groaned.

'Never mind, we'll do it tomorrow. Ruffy, do you want to fall right through the hole and into the sea?' Paras remarked, pulling the sniffing dog back with a laugh.

Ruffy sure showed a lot of guts, leaning dangerously over the hole. Vijju held him by the collar to restrain him.

'I say,' Tina spoke suddenly and her voice was a little queer. 'Come to the window, quick.'

The urgency in her voice, made them hasten toward the window.

'What is it?' Fulki whispered.

Tina pointed down the cliff. Jain was slowly trudging up the hill. Every now and then, he would stop and place something before his eyes, scouring the landscape with it, but mostly focussing on the cottage.

'Binoculars,' Samir said flatly. 'He's examining the house with his binoculars...which means he will be able to spot us. Quick.'

But it was too late. Jain had already seen the children through his binoculars. He held them trained on their window, closely observing their reactions. Samir pulled them all back hastily into the room and away from the window.

'But what is he *doing*?' Tina frowned. '*Spying* on the cottage?'

'Hardly. I think, he must have gone bird watching somewhere and on his way back was perhaps casually studying the cottage,' Paras guessed.

Tina shook her head. 'What a creepy fellow... First the pistol and now this....'

'Pistol?' Vijju stared from one to the other and they had to tell him.

'But don't breathe a word of this to anyone, not even Panna. For all we know, it may be something harmless,' Fulki explained and Vijju nodded in agreement.

'Come on, it's a beautiful evening, let's go down to the beach for a walk,' Samir suggested and Ruffy at once woofed in agreement.

The weather was lovely outside, with the sun gliding down over the sea, splashing it with a golden colour. The wind had picked up, blowing their hair helter-skelter. The children enjoyed their walk and returned home with their stomachs growling.

Across to Malabar Island

The next morning, the children went back to the deserted cove to bathe. They ran all the way down, the wind buffeting against their bodies. It was fun to plunge into the water and jump with the rolling waves.

'This is great!' Samir shouted, as he swam further out with strong strokes.

All of them were good swimmers, especially Samir and Tina. They had won several competitions and were very proud of it.

They played games in the water, swimming under and catching each other's feet. It certainly was fun! Diving deep and coming up again, somersaulting like ducks.

'I don't want to get out, it's so lovely,' Fulki sighed when it was time to leave.

'But we must because I'm ravenous. Come on everyone, out of the water on the double!' Tina used her imperious, class monitor voice and the others obeyed with a grin.

After breakfast, the children decided to explore the passage in the girls' room. Excitement streaked through them as Vijju opened the trap door.

'No Ruffy, not you. You will go tearing down the stairs and land hard on the ground. Go down to the beach and meet us there. Good dog Ruffy, you understand, don't you?' Vijju spoke to his dog.

Ruffy sure did because he raced out of the room.

'He can understand every word you speak,' Fulki said, in wonder. 'Do you take him to school with you?'

The boy shook his head. 'No, though I go to a local school. It's terrible to leave him for a whole day. We miss each other a lot but then, I make up for it every evening.'

The others felt sorry for him. It was obvious that Vijju was very attached to Ruffy. It must be miserable for them, not to be with each other all the time. Still it was better than a boarding school. At least they spent the rest of the time together.

'Ready, all? I'll go down first and you four follow me. But please, be careful because these steps are steep and slippery. And when I ask you to stop, you must stop at once,' Vijju instructed.

The gloomy darkness in the hole looked frightening but there was also a sense of adventure in it. Vijju lowered himself into the hole. The torch light fell on the first step and he slowly ventured further down the passage. Paras went in after him, followed by the girls and Samir in the end. The passage was narrow and winding, and the children had to bend their heads low, as they carefully tread on the gradually descending steep steps. They felt very excited, it was better than the secret room. It was almost like a long tunnel, with its damp air and musty smell of unuse.

They continued single file for a few minutes and then suddenly Vijju halted without warning. Paras bumped into him, his glasses almost falling off and so did the others in quick succession.

'Ouch!' Paras clutched on to his glasses. 'What an ass you are! Why didn't you say "stop"?'

'Sorry,' Vijju grinned sheepishly in the darkness. 'I didn't see the rope myself. I'm going down. So please hold the torch and be careful all of you. It's quite a jump at the end of the rope.'

Very smoothly he slid down the rope and into ankle-deep pool of water. One by one the others did the same, sliding cautiously down the rope. They were in a cave now but sunlight filtered in through the opening.

'This is a small passage which joins the cove. If you go right, you will find my red boat. But we cannot go this way, since the water is waist-deep. The way on the left leads to the beach.'

They made their way out in the open and were immediately met with loud, joyous barks.

'Woof, woof!' Ruffy threw himself on Vijju, his tail wagging wildly.

'Good dog, Ruffy! We didn't take too long, did we?' Samir patted him.

Ruffy licked his hand and ran ahead. 'I'm feeling so thirsty. Let's go to the beach and have some *nariyal pani,* shall we?' Fulki suggested.

There was a unanimous chorus of agreement. So while Samir and Paras went to buy the coconuts, the girls and Vijju relaxed on the beach. Soon all of them were sipping coconut water with Ruffy swallowing huge licks from a very special ice-cream cup.

'I would love to go on a picnic. The weather is ideal for one. Can't we go somewhere?' Tina wondered.

'Oh yes, let's row across to Malabar Island. It will be fun to look at the castle. I've never seen one. Is it dangerous Vijju? I mean, the parts don't fall off, do they?' Samir asked.

'No, the island is a perfect spot for a picnic. Ruffy and I go there often, taking our lunch with us,' Vijju fondled the dog's head affectionately.

'Then we should plan one and go, shall we? Panna might arrange a nice food basket for us. I'm getting excited and restless at the mere prospect!' Paras grinned. 'Can we borrow your boat? Or better still, why don't you accompany us?'

Vijju shrugged. 'I doubt if I can come with you today, what with more guests arriving. But you may of course use my boat.'

'That's really decent of you,' Samir smiled, his dimple deepening.

'And I'm sure Panna will be glad to get rid of us for the day, unless of course, she needs our help,' Tina said.

But Panna did not need their help. And she was glad they would be out of the way. She handed them a freshly baked piece of chocolate cake.

'Can we take Vijju along with us Panna?' Fulki asked, munching the delicious cake.

'Oh no, dear, I shall need Vijju to run some errands for me. But you may certainly take Ruffy with you. I would hate it if he upsets any of the guests.'

The children looked at Vijju who hid his disappointment, '*Aai* is right. I shall have to be around here, but Ruffy will feel cooped up and miserable. So please, take him, he'll be as good as gold with you. Won't you, Ruffy?'

'Woof!' the dog responded readily and Samir stroked his shiny black coat.

'We'd love to take Ruffy with us. Would you like to come with us, Ruffy?'

Once again the dog replied with enthusiasm, 'Woof, woof!' and the children laughed.

'Wonderful doggie! You do understand every word we speak!' Tina fondled him behind the ears. Ruffy thumped his tail on the floor and cocked his head on one side as if in agreement.

After lunch, Samir insisted on making the sandwiches himself much to Panna's amazement. She watched him as he deftly applied layers of homemade white butter, mango pickles and tomatoes and cucumbers to the slices. He offered Panna a sandwich and was thrilled when she exclaimed at the taste. Then, feeling extremely satisfied he raced to the beach, while the girls helped Panna pack their picnic snacks—sandwiches, chocolate cakes, coconut barfi, and a big bottle of mango juice along with some fresh mangoes too! The basket was overflowing, as the girls carried it between them to the deserted cove. The boys had already pulled out the boat.

'Goodbye and enjoy your picnic,' Vijju gave a wan smile as they all got into the boat, placing the basket between their feet. 'Be careful when you approach the island, there are many rocks around and you could graze the boat.'

'Don't worry, we'll be careful,' Samir promised.

He and Vijju pushed the boat into the water. Then Samir jumped in and took the oar. They waved to Vijju as the boat glided smoothly into the sea. Ruffy watched his master on the shore and gave a few wistful barks.

'Don't look so sad, Ruffy dear, you're going to meet him in a few hours from now,' Fulki patted him fondly.

Samir and Paras rowed strongly and steadily and the boat moved effortlessly in the water. It was hot and the children were glad they were wearing caps. The wind fanned and cooled their red faces. Fulki ran her hand through the water. This was fun! They have never had such lovely holidays before. Swimming, boating, exploring, picnicking, and lazing around...and what could possibly be more exciting than secret passages? Mama had been right when she had said that this was the right place for their holidays.

'Let me take the oar, Paras. I'd like to try my hand at it,' Tina suggested and her brother readily relinquished his oar to her.

But when Fulki suggested the same idea, Samir seemed a little doubtful, 'Are you sure you can? I mean, it's tough and....'

'Samir, give her the oar,' Tina remarked patiently and Samir grinned. He loved to pull his younger sister's leg.

The girls proved to be good rowers and the boys were glad to rest their arms. Ruffy was as excited as the children and he moved restlessly in the small space. The boat rocked unsteadily and finally, Samir had to hold him firmly by the collar. The island was slowly becoming gigantic in size. The sound of birds reached their ears, as they drew closer and closer. Remembering Vijju's warning, the boys took over the oars, carefully avoiding the rocks. They skilfully manoeuvred the boat, keeping a sharp look for the cove.

A tall building of old, crumpled stone loomed largely from the centre of the island and the children gazed in amazement at the huge structure.

'Doesn't the castle look a little sinister?' Fulki's voice held a sense of awe.

Birds were soaring and circling the castle top. The children watched fascinated, as they let the boat float for a while.

'It appears mysterious and somewhat spooky. I can't imagine being left down in the dungeons there, without food and water or perhaps even proper light.' Paras shivered at the thought.

'Then don't imagine it,' Tina said, practically. 'We don't have to explore the dungeons. We can have a lovely picnic on the island and enjoy ourselves with pleasant thoughts.'

The boys took the oars again and they rowed steadily. Suddenly, the cove appeared in sight.

'There it is! Yay! We've finally arrived, I'm so excited!' Fulki exclaimed, rocking the boat in her eagerness.

'Hey careful,' Samir warned, but everyone shared her feeling. Even Ruffy barked in anticipation.

'Malabar Island, here we come. I hope you have a good welcome ready for us!' Fulki sang out.

'Don't be silly.' Paras grinned.

The sun hid behind the clouds as the boat touched the cove. But as the children dragged the boat up to safety, it came out again, beating down on them in full glory.

A Picnic At The Castle

The children pulled the boat further up into the sandy cove, which was a sheltered beach enclosed within rocks, and tied it firmly to a jutting rock.

'I think it ought to be okay here,' Samir said, as he rechecked the rope. He picked up the heavy food basket and the girls took the *chatais* which they had brought along to sit on. 'Ruffy, lead the way. You know this island, don't you?'

'Woof!' was the dog's immediate response.

He set out at once, leading them up a stony path, climbing and jumping up to the top of the island. The children followed, a little slowly. They were used to outdoor activity and this was not very difficult. The island was beautiful. Fresh green tufts of grass sprouted like uneven carpet on the ground and in between rocks. Pools of water glistened between the gaps and there was even a small spring which trickled down to the beach. The breeze became stronger as they climbed higher and higher, their faces red and chests puffing.

'Whew! It *is* hot today. Do you think it might rain?' Tina panted, glancing up at the cloudy sky.

'It may,' Samir shielded his eyes to look up at the sky.

They climbed after Ruffy who turned around occasionally, waiting impatiently for them to catch up. As they approached the top, the castle came in view again. It was certainly one huge ruin, massive and falling in pieces from all the sides. But in its hey days it must have been a glorious structure of pomp and ceremony. Now, only a tall, solitary tower rose like a lone survivor, standing erect, daring the scorching heat of the day.

'The iron gate has worn off,' Paras observed. The two iron poles, which represented the gates, stood wide apart, looking forlorn and bare.

They stood on the top of the island and gazed in astonishment. What a splendid view! Miles of calm, blue sea surrounded them as far as the eye could see.

'Isn't it breathtaking?' Fulki exclaimed. 'We can even see the cottage quite clearly.'

Sure enough the cottage appeared quite near, in spite of the great distance. It was a huge speck on the hill opposite the island. The island stretched on both the sides, green and rocky, interspersed with mango and coconut trees.

'There isn't much to explore here. I can see no caves and we can see the whole island from this spot,' Tina said, her two plaits standing out against the wind.

'There's the castle to explore. I think that should be exciting enough for the day.' Samir placed the heavy basket of food down and flexed his arm. 'Hey, where's Ruffy? He was here a moment ago!'

As if in response, they heard Ruffy's muffled bark.

'I think he's inside the castle. Well, let's go and examine it thoroughly before we have something to eat,' Paras suggested.

The others agreed and began climbing the steps to the door-less entrance. It was a little dark inside after the blaring sunshine and much cooler. As their eyes got accustomed to the darkness, they noticed that they were in a sort of low room. A door led to another dark room and then to an open courtyard. Ruffy bounded towards them. He had been busy sniffing the corners. Many parts of the roof and walls had fallen in and there seemed very little of the castle left. But the tower attracted the children a great deal.

'It's like a magnet in these ruins,' Samir observed. 'Have you noticed how the birds hover round the tower?'

'Kites,' supplied Tina, knowledgeably. 'We ought to be very careful while eating. Kites have a nasty habit of snatching food straight off your hands!'

'Look, there's a staircase at the side of the courtyard. I think it must lead to the tower. Should we try it?' Fulki pointed to a spiral staircase, in the good part of the courtyard.

'Yes, but first I'm keeping this basket here. No point carrying that heavy thing right to the top,' Samir sighed. 'Come on, Ruffy, to the tower. You don't want to be left behind, do you?'

Ruffy joined them at once, his tail wagging. The staircase looked rather narrow and winded up like a ribbon.

'I do hope it is safe,' Samir frowned.

'I think not. It looks so rickety and dangerous. Just imagine, what if a step breaks right in the centre and we all crash through, straight to the bottom,' Paras contemplated, solemnly.

Fulki looked so alarmed that Tina intervened smoothly, 'You are filled with morbid thoughts today, aren't you, Paras? The staircase is perfectly safe, I'm sure. Vijju would have warned us otherwise,' she said, logically. 'Anyway, Ruffy is already half way up the steps. He must have been up in the tower several times with Vijju. Come on, let's follow him.'

Fulki made a face at Paras who pulled her ample curls in a brotherly manner. They had to climb single file, holding on to the railing. It was slow progress and the children were careful not to look down. They tested each step, just to be on the safe side, even though Ruffy bounded up spiritedly.

The journey came to an end at last, in a small passage which led to a door on the right. Samir tried to turn the knob and it opened very smoothly. It was a small room with a window. Cobwebs hung from the wall and a thick layer of dust covered the floor. The children moved to the window and opened it. Immediately a strong blast of wind slapped them forcefully in the face, almost overthrowing them. The view was amazing!

'We are almost touching the sky,' Samir said, in awe.

Ruffy pattered to the window and placing his legs on the sill, pushed his head out. The hair of his thick coat, stood out like mane and he seemed to completely enjoy the gasping breeze.

'Hey, you don't want to fall off, do you?' Samir placed a restraining hand on the dog.

'Woof!' he said and the children laughed.

The strong wind slapped their faces and tugged savagely at their hair, as they stood gazing out at the open sea. The birds were flying low, circling the tower and crying out loudly. Ruffy was so startled at the sound that he withdrew immediately.

'You can't be frightened of birds, silly, they are only birds,' Fulki explained.

Ruffy wagged his tail in understanding, but he preferred to leave. He stood by the door, looking at them expectantly.

'Okay, we're coming,' Paras grinned. 'In any case, I wouldn't mind eating now.'

The others agreed. Their stomachs were rumbling in anticipation of the lovely feast Panna had packed for them. Ruffy led the way hastily. He knew that there was a boiled egg and some chicken in the basket for him and he was excited. One by one the children descended the spiral staircase. Once down, they heaved a sigh of relief. They were feeling giddy with the continuous circular motion.

They carried the food outside and chose a lovely, grassy spot. Paras unfolded the *chatais* and Tina laid out the food. Ruffy impatiently sniffed at the packets, poking them with his nose and Tina had to push him away.

'Hold on, Ruffy, you've got to be patient. Here, take your food, you greedy dog! Go and sit there, I said *there*!'

But Ruffy settled down beside her and concentrated on his meal. Finally, Tina gave up.

'Wow! Samir, you have outdone yourself. What delicious sandwiches!' Paras acknowledged.

'Yes, they are really good,' Fulki agreed.

'Thanks, I try to make every dish from my heart.' Samir smiled, looking pleased.

The children tucked into the delicious spread, chatting about everything. Especially, about Jain and his pistol. But apart from their suspicions, there was nothing really concrete for them to fall on, so the conversation dwindled.

'I don't think I much like the look of those kites,' Fulki said. 'Let's cover up the food.'

They covered up the packets with haste. A great many kites were suddenly flying rather low. The children eyed them warily, as they ate. Suddenly, as quick as lightening, and before Samir could wink, a kite scooped down and snatched his sandwich away! The children were stunned. Ruffy started barking and began chasing the bird in vain for it was already a speck in the sky.

'Wow! That was beautifully done,' Samir exclaimed. 'It's no use, Ruffy, the bird's gone and finished my sandwich by now. So, stop creating a racket.'

'I had warned you,' Tina said, placidly. 'Now, I vote we carry the food inside and eat peacefully. I can see some more kites heading our way.'

The others needed no coaxing. One incident was enough for them to realise that they were dealing with a lot of expertise. They sat at the door-less entrance, with the food placed well inside the room. Ruffy took his place on the lower step, as if on guard. In no time the children were pleased to see the birds vanishing into the sky.

'Well, that was a narrow miss. I am still a bit shaken with that close encounter,' Samir admitted, sheepishly.

'Hey look, there's a boat heading this way!' Paras pointed out.

Ruffy stood up at once, his ears straight and barking at nothing in particular.

'Oh, do be quiet, Ruffy. It's only some people, picnickers like us, coming to see the island and the castle,' Tina said. 'Looks like a motorboat. I can hear the sound'.

They all heard it. Rrr…rr…rr… It was steady and low, and the children saw the boat land smoothly in the cove. Two figures got out and after a while began climbing up the hill.

'Goodness, it's six already. Get up lazybones and begin packing,' Tina said.

The others got up with a sigh. It was such a beautiful evening they could sit here forever. But they had to leave before it got too dark. Slowly, they repacked the leftover food in the basket. They were so busy picking up the litter, that they did not notice the two men approaching them. It was when Ruffy suddenly began barking, that Samir placed a hand on his collar and stared at the strangers. He gasped in recognition. They were the same men who had driven them off the road!

'Calm down, Ruffy. It's okay,' he patted the dog, his eyes following the men.

'Hello kids!' the man in the red kurta spoke to them. Today, he had worn jeans instead of a lungi. 'Nice dog.'

The children glanced at each other, not knowing how to respond.

'Are you picnicking here?' the man asked again, his small eyes sweeping over them.

'Yes,' Samir replied.

'Do you by any chance know the way to the dungeons? I heard that they are very interesting,' his thin lips twisted in a smile.

The bald man was silent, fiddling nervously with a silver watch strap.

'No, I'm afraid not,' Samir replied. Ruffy had stopped barking, but his deep growls were a steady background music.

'Well, never mind. See you then. Come on!' he gestured to the bald man who followed him meekly inside the castle.

'Let's go, I don't feel like hanging around here anymore,' Fulki shivered.

'Right. Stop it, Ruffy, they are gone and we are going home too,' Paras said.

They began climbing down to the cove, talking in low voices. What were these two men doing here, this late? To visit the dungeons in the dark? Rather strange taste they had.

The sun was beginning to go down over the sea as the children reached the cove. The men's' motorboat was parked on the sand. It was multi-coloured and loaded with rugs and packets of food.

'Look at that stuff. Those two seem to be planning a party here,' Samir frowned.

'In the dungeons? Hardly!' Tina remarked.

The boys untied their boat and pushed it into the water. 'Everybody aboard! You too, Ruffy. No more exploring. Push, Paras, and jump!'

Paras gave a big shove and jumped into the boat, taking the oar at once. The sea was blue-green, the waves rippling in the golden sheen of the setting sun. As they rowed skilfully and energetically past the rocks, the children saw the birds circling the tower.

'Goodbye Malabar Island and Castle!' Fulki sang out. 'We had a lovely time, thank you!'

She waved out to the island and the others did the same. Ruffy gave a loud, conclusive 'Woof!' as the boat glided farther and farther into the sea.

6

Guests At The Cottage

The sinking sun was throwing rainbow colours on the sea, as the boys rowed steadily. Tina looked thoughtful, as her eyes screened the island.

'They haven't returned to the cove yet,' she said, finally.

'Who?' Paras asked, surprised.

'Those two men. I think they plan to stay the night, which is a little queer, isn't it?' Tina remarked.

'Unless they wish to explore the dungeons in the dark, to experience the real effect,' Samir said.

Fulki shivered, 'Spooky!'

'It's strange if they really spend the night on the island. They didn't look roofless or stranded and they certainly didn't appear to be picnickers. Why should they want to spend the night there? We did see the boat filled with supplies, didn't we?' Tina pondered.

'I'll tell you what we can do. Let's loiter around on the beach and see if the motorboat returns or passes us. That way, we'll know for sure if they stayed the night,' Paras suggested.

'Right,' Tina agreed.

As they approached the mainland, Samir said, 'I say, we quite forgot about the high tide. The water must be well into the cove now. We won't be able to tie the boat in the usual place.' He looked dismayed.

The others were thoughtful. No one had thought about this problem. They were in a fix. They couldn't possibly tie the boat in the deserted cove. The sun had set and a cool breeze was blowing, making the children shiver.

'We'll have to leave it on the beach,' Tina said, finally. 'And hope for the best. Come on, it's quite dark.'

They rowed past the cove and headed towards the beach. Finally, the boat scraped the sand and the children tugged it hard and higher up the beach, away from the water. Fulki caught sight of some rocks farther ahead.

'Those rocks look like a perfectly safe place for the boat,' she pointed to the rocks. 'Though, it's going to require all our strength to pull it up there!'

'Give a big heave all of you. One, two, three!' Samir encouraged and the children pushed and pulled with all their strength. Ruffy ran around them, wondering what they were up to, as they managed to secure the boat to the rocks.

'Whew! That was some job!' Paras sighed, pressing his aching arms.

Just then they heard the distant roar of a motor. The children looked at each other expectantly.

'I think it's them!' Samir whispered. 'Come on, let's go see if we can figure out anything in the dark.'

They stood on the beach with the cold wind stinging their faces. Their feet were wet and they shivered in the night's dampness. Ruffy gave a loud bark, not understanding what they were up to. Finally, thoroughly bored, he headed towards the cottage on his own.

The beach was isolated and the moon was shining brilliantly, forming silver lines on the murky sea.

'Look, there it is! It is heading straight on,' Paras exclaimed.

The dark shape of the boat was heading in the opposite direction. The children could see only one man at the helm and there was no sign of the other one.

As the boat vanished into the dark, Tina commented, 'So one of them *has* stayed back on the island. I wonder why.'

'It is rather strange, isn't it?' Samir mused, as they retraced their steps towards the cottage. 'I can't think of any earthly reason to spend a night alone on a lonely island.'

'Well, Panna must be wondering where we've vanished. And those two new guests must have arrived by now,' Paras remembered.

'Doesn't anyone have a torch here? I stumbled twice in the dark,' Fulki grumbled.

Fortunately, Samir had a torch with him and he shone it on the rough ground. They climbed up the hill as fast they could, wondering what Panna would say. She would certainly be worried to see Ruffy turning up without them.

Panna *was* worried but not angry and readily forgave the children. 'Now, you four had better rush in and wash up. You must be tired with all that rowing and dinner is waiting. So, hurry up!'

'Right!' Samir grinned. 'Panna, have the guests arrived yet?'

'Oh yes, Sagar*ji* is in his room and Mrs Fernando has gone for a long walk. Jain must be around somewhere.'.

The children climbed up wearily to their rooms, their legs suddenly feeling like a ton of bricks. A wash was just what they needed. Within half an hour, they were scrubbed and sparkling, feeling totally refreshed. They trooped down to the dining room, their spirits up again and wondering about the new arrivals to the cottage. If they were anything like Jain, the atmosphere in the cottage would certainly be most gloomy.

An oldish lady was sitting at the table. She had a grey bob and square glasses covered her eyes. She was plump and dressed in a long, printed frock. Mrs Fernando, Fulki thought as she smiled at them.

'Hello, children!' she greeted, in a sweet voice and a pleasant smile on her face. 'I am Mrs Fernando. I believe you are here on your holidays? This is a great place, isn't it?'

The children sat around the table, a little shy.

'Yes,' Tina returned the polite smile. 'We have enjoyed every single day since we arrived.' She set up an instant conversation, introducing each of her cousins. She was very good at talking to strangers and Paras secretly admired this quality of hers.

'You're a nature writer, aren't you?' Tina continued. 'I confess, I'm not much of a reader of such books, but you must be famous in your circle.'

Mrs Fernando nodded. 'Yes, a nature writer. And quite comfortably popular—which means that I don't get mobbed in the streets.' She giggled.

Panna was placing bowls of rice and prawn curry on the table, with fresh fried pomfret.

'Where are Vijju and Ruffy?' Fulki asked.

'Oh, he's tied up that tiresome dog. He wouldn't stop barking at Mrs Fernando,' Panna explained with a sigh.

'I am terrified of dogs,' the new guest admitted, ruefully. 'And the feeling is mutual, because they don't seem to like me as well. Which is a pity, I would have liked to be friends with Ruffy, that's his name, isn't it?'

'You folks can begin your meal, I shall just hop up and call the other two. Sagar*ji* began his work immediately after he arrived and I'm sure he's forgotten that he's got to eat as well! And as for Jain*ji*....' Panna shrugged as if she had no words to describe the man.

She left the room, as the others tucked into the mouth-watering meal. Between mouthfuls, Samir enquired, 'Did you enjoy your walk this evening?'

'Oh yes! I walked right till the other village—Ranpar village—I believe it's the far end where there is a nice cove for the boats. Have you been there? You must see it. And I also intend going to that island in the middle of the sea. I saw a great many kites circling the tower of the castle....'

Mrs Fernando was interrupted by the arrival of Mr Sagar, who bustled into the dining room, looking most disgruntled. The Desai children glanced up to observe a man of medium height, on the thinner side, with a grey-white French beard and rather unkempt hair. His intelligent eyes stared at the children from behind, well-polished glasses. Surprise was written all over his face as he raised his thick eyebrows.

'Children? Panna, I thought you said there would be no children and that I could work in peace,' he remarked with a scowl.

'I said no such thing.' Panna firmly propelled him into a chair. 'In fact, I did warn you that there would be children and you said it did not matter. You've just forgotten, as usual. And don't worry, they won't create a racket or any such thing. Now, enjoy your meal.'

Mr Sagar did not need further coaxing. Much to the children's surprise, he was a tremendous eater. He emptied plate after plate, chatting continuously and cheerfully. The children lost their bashfulness, as he shot questions at them and listened with genuine interest. In the middle of the meal, Jain joined them without a word and Panna made the introductions. The two men exchanged some polite words and then Mr Sagar continued chatting with the children.

Mrs Fernando was an interested listener, as she contributed with her titbits. But Jain maintained an absolute silence, eating his food with a quiet relish. Finally, the meal was over and the children realised that they had actually enjoyed the company.

Mrs Fernando stifled a yawn. 'I'm retiring for the night. Goodnight, everyone.'

'Goodnight, I think I will be going out for a short walk,' Mr Sagar announced and the children were surprised.

A walk? At this time of the night?

'If you don't mind, I would like to join you,' Jain spoke up, suddenly.

The children stared at him. What a strange suggestion from someone who hadn't spoken a word during the meal. Even Sagar*ji* looked a little surprised.

'Er…sure. Let's go.'

The two men left the dining room and Tina glanced meaningfully at the others. Thoughts flitted through her brain at lightning speed. What did this mean? Why was Jain going out of the way to accompany the scientist? Did he still have his pistol with him? What if he used it? What if he harmed Sagar*ji*? Something was not right, but she could not understand it.

They climbed to their bedrooms, talking in muted tones. Since none of them were feeling sleepy, they sat in the girls' room and chatted about the guests. A little later Vijju also joined them with Ruffy in tow. It was when Fulki picked up the pillow to hold it on her lap, that she noticed the piece of paper beneath it. Puzzled, she unfolded the small slip and stared in astonishment.

'Listen to this!' her voice croaked. 'GO BACK HOME! THIS PLACE IS DANGEROUS!'

The others crowded near her, sheer amazement written on their faces. Samir took the paper from his sister.

'A computer print-out,' he remarked, instantly. 'But what does it mean?'

'Someone is trying to warn you off,' Vijju said. 'But why? Malabar Cottage is one of the safest places in the world!'

'Of course, it is!' Tina spoke up. 'Someone is simply trying to frighten us off. And if not, it is a very stupid prank.'

'But who and why would anyone do such a thing?' Paras questioned, nudging his glasses up the nose.

'Excuse me a minute,' Samir said, suddenly. He leapt off the bed and slipped out of the room.

'Now, what is *he* up to?' Paras wondered.

'There's something really queer about this warning note,' Fulki read the words again. 'As if it wasn't written to frighten us but to warn us. It's obvious that someone doesn't want us here.'

'The question is—is it a friendly warning or a threat? You know the kind—go back home or else, kind of threat,' Tina wondered.

Samir returned just then, a self-pleased smile lighting up his face. 'My guess proved right. This *is* a computer print-out. And guess who has a laptop here?'

'I should say all three would have one—if they are the advanced types. One a businessman, the other a scientist and the third, a writer,' Paras replied.

'Yes, but only two of them have a printer,' Samir emphasised. 'Jain and Sagar. I quickly checked their rooms, just now. Luckily, they were not locked. Now, the question is which one of them wrote that note?'

The children were thoughtful. Why would either of the men place such a strange note on their bed? And did he really expect them to take him seriously and go back home in the midst of their wonderful holidays?

'Perhaps there will be more of such notes,' Fulki predicted. 'I mean, whoever wrote this may want to explain himself and tell us why this place is dangerous.'

'No harm waiting and watching of course,' Samir agreed.

Vijju gave a big yawn and immediately Ruffy copied him. That set the children off, one after the other.

'That does it. I'm off to bed!' Paras stretched. 'We can ponder over this problem in the morning.'

The others agreed and the boys dispersed. Tina and Fulki stayed awake in their beds, talking in whispers but sleep took over gradually.

'You know, I've been thinking for a while,' Tina said. 'Something about what Fernando said during dinner. It did not strike me as odd then, but now when I think of it, I realise that it isn't possible. She couldn't have... Fulki...Fulki?'

But Fulki was fast asleep. Tina smiled and turned on her side.

Within minutes all the children had slipped into a deep slumber, dreaming of castles, islands, secret passages and, of course, warning notes.

The Investigation and Gopal Kutty

The day dawned into a rather dull one. The sky was cloudy, the air was stuffy and the heat was stifling. After breakfast the first thing the children did was to row the boat back to the cove. Vijju had told them the boat could be rowed through the small passage to the cove and Samir and Paras carried out the plan. The passage was quite low and they had to bend their heads so as not to bang them against the rocky roof. It was narrow too and the boys felt as if they were in a small tunnel. They tied the boat in the usual place and swam out to where the girls were splashing in the water.

'What do we do today?' Fulki wondered. 'It's such a dull day.'

'Why don't we go to the village and meet Panna's mother? She promised to tell us about Pilot-Eye, didn't she?' Tina suggested.

'That's a good idea,' Paras agreed.

'I can also ask her if she has any unique spices to sell,' Samir said.

'And we can walk down to Ranpar village too and see the beautiful cove Mrs Fernando was talking about,' Fulki suggested.

'We should ask Panna if she wants us to buy anything from the village,' added Tina, already stepping out of the water.

They all dried themselves and ran up the cliff to the cottage. Panna was dusting the house and was pleased when she heard that they were going down to the village.

'Good, I need some groceries and I'll make you a list in a jiffy.' She dropped the duster in a chair and hurried to the kitchen.

In the meanwhile, the children quickly changed into fresh pairs of jeans and rain jackets. As they came down, Panna was ready with a big shopping bag and a list which she handed to Samir.

'Here it is. I hope you know my mother's shop? You do—good, you needn't pay her, just order these things and ask her to treat you to some juice. And yes, on your way out, you can pluck some ripe mangoes which you can suck on your way to the village.' She smiled.

'Wow! Thanks, Panna, we'd love that,' the children chorused and Panna beamed.

The mango tree in the garden was laden with yellow-orange, succulently shaped fruits, ready to be plucked and devoured. The children spent the next half hour, climbing the trees and dropping the mangoes into the waiting arms of the others. Soon a dozen delicious fruits were collected and the children sucked them merrily. It was really fun. Eating mangoes straight off the trees was a divine experience. Finally, satiated, they began their journey down the hill and to the grocery store.

Panna's mother was serving a customer when they trooped into the dark, cool and cramped store. She smiled at them warmly, finished with the customer and turned to them.

'Good to see you again,' she beamed, her face breaking into a thousand wrinkles.

As she chatted, she began weighing out the ingredients mentioned in the list. The children watched her amazed, as she found stuff kept in the darkest of corners, without even looking.

'You've been to the island, haven't you? Ah… and the castle…it's very old…seen many a terrible happenings.' The old lady kept the parcel she was holding on the counter and lowered her voice. 'The dungeons of the castle, particularly, saw some horrible things—people, mostly the over-smart types wanting to catch the smugglers, landed up in those dungeons—no one knew how or when,' she chuckled, a reminiscent gleam in her eye.

The children listened attentively. They had heard this story from Vijju of course, but it was thrilling to hear the old lady talk about it—almost as if it was from an eye-witness! She was now warming up to the conversation and they were eager to hear more of her tales.

'Who was Pilot-Eye?' Tina asked.

'Pilot-Eye… He was the ring leader of the gang. That wasn't his real name, of course. But he had a black patch on his right eye and a thick beard and moustache to hide his real identity. That's why he was called Pilot-Eye by all. Well, a catchy name which certainly suited him. He would smuggle goods into the country via the sea and he was stinking rich. But he was also a good man with a heart of gold. You could have asked any of the poor men and women around—they swore by him and worshipped the ground he tread on. He helped them with money and goods and saw that no one starved—that was why nobody ever spoke against him. Only his enemies—or the smart and greedy ones interested in the enormous prize money on his head, tried to catch him and then *they* were never seen again. Everyone *guessed* where they were but no one *knew*. Or well, at least they *pretended* not to know. In those days it was impossible to reach the island by night because of the steep, treacherous rocks. And yet, he managed to take the prisoners to the dungeons. Of course, since he owned the cottage, it was easy for him.'

'You mean Malabar Cottage actually belonged to him? He lived there?' Fulki's eyes opened wide.

Panna's mother nodded. 'My great-great-grandfather and he jointly owned the cottage. My great-grandmother would secretly watch them every night, not knowing what was really happening. But one night, she saw the body of a man—all gagged and tied, and she screamed. Her father spanked her real hard and ordered her off to her room. But she *did* overhear them say that they would take the man by the *secret tunnel*!'

The children gasped. So it was true! There *really* was a tunnel hidden somewhere in the area. Panna's mother was so engrossed in her tale that she spilled some sugar into the balance. She glanced at it, surprised that such a thing should happen.

'Does it mean that the tunnel starts somewhere near the cottage and goes right up to the island?' Samir asked, his eyes bright. He had forgotten all about asking the old woman about spices and herbs.

'Oh yes, but I've no idea where it is. As a girl I tried my best to hunt for it and so did Panna and Vijju. But we all have been unlucky.' She shook her head sadly.

'We're going to help Vijju look for it,' Paras volunteered and the old lady smiled.

'Good, he needs the help. I hope you will be luckier than me. And when you do find it, let me know at once and I shall explore it with you.'

The children laughed at the idea. They could well imagine Panna's mother waddling through a dark, musty and long-lost tunnel. She was perfectly capable!

'Here's the bag with all the items. Panna does require a lot of stuff, doesn't she? With suddenly so many guests flooding her little cottage, it's no wonder. If you want to go to the beach, you can leave the bag here and pick it up later.'

Since Samir was about to make the same suggestion, they accepted and walked out of the dark shop into the cloudy, stuffy day. A weak breeze was blowing and the children fanned themselves with kerchiefs, as they strolled across the tiny village. It comprised a few houses with red, tiled sloping roofs, a quaint post-office and a school. They ambled aimlessly along the sandy lanes, lined with coconut and mango trees, with fruits swinging from the branches.

'Let's go and see that cove, shall we?' Tina suggested. 'Perhaps we just may find that motorboat there.'

The idea spurted them into a brisk trot, reminding them forcefully of all the strange happenings since they had arrived. They kept to the beach, occasionally removing their shoes and walking along the edge of the water. Ranpar village was farther than they had expected but the long walk was worth it. The village was larger than theirs and more commercially oriented with advertising banners and films posters. There was even a small mobile theatre in a huge tent, showing an old Hindi film. The children were amused as a knot of people slid the flap aside and slipped into their seats on the floor.

Paras bought some *nariyal pani* since all of them were thirsty. Sipping the coconut water, they headed towards the cove, set between two cliffs. The sea was still and calm, and as blue as the sky. An array of bright, multicoloured boats in all sizes aligned the beach.

'This seems to be a regular stop for boats. And look at the number of huts there, they look so lovely!' Fulki exclaimed.

It *was* very picturesque. Thatched huts stood amongst tall, swaying coconut trees on a hill. Colourful fishing nets were hung out on old boats on the slopes and it was obvious that fishermen lived in the huts.

The children walked along the cove, running their hands over the boats, trying to spot the one they had seen at the island. And sure enough, there it stood, a little comical-looking with its butterfly stripes.

'So, the two men *did* hire a boat from here. And if one of the men returned with the boat, then the other has no means of leaving the island,' Fulki remarked.

'Surely that isn't a kind of prediction, is it?' Samir teased.

'Of course not! It's common sense.' Fulki rounded on him hotly, her curls bobbing.

'Okay, you two,' Tina broke in, hastily. 'Samir, we've decided not to poke fun at Fulki, haven't we?'

'*You* have decided,' Samir pointed out. 'You were so taken up by her gun prediction that you thought her every word would be prophetic. Fulki and her crystal!'

'Now, now…' It was Paras's turn to stop the squabbling. 'Are we going to go ahead with our investigation or are you….'

But Fulki was angry with her brother. 'Okay, I'll soon predict something and if it comes true, you will have to apologise to my crystal.'

'Accepted, only don't take too long to predict that *something*.' Samir laughed

'You two are impossible.' Tina shook her head in exasperation. 'I'm going to try and find out who hired this boat. Is anyone interested?'

'I am,' Samir answered, promptly.

'But what do we want their names for?' Paras asked, puzzled.

'You never know, the information may prove handy.' Samir grinned.

They went up to the wooden shack, which seemed to be a make-shift office. A man clad in a lungi and a vest, sat writing on a rickety wooden table. As the children approached him, he looked up enquiringly.

'Yes?'

'Er...we needed some information,' Samir spoke in Marathi. 'There is a striped boat outside which two men hired yesterday. Could you please tell us their names?'

The man stared at them curiously, from behind thick glasses. 'And why do you need this information?'

For a moment Samir looked floored, glancing at the others. But he recovered quickly, 'Well, actually we met them on the island yesterday and chatted with them, but forgot to ask them their names. Just now, while we were strolling, we caught sight of the boat and realised that you could probably help us?' Samir explained.

The perfect truth and the others couldn't help admiring him.

The man nodded, satisfied. He opened a worn-out register and peered through the pages, running a grubby finger down the list of names. 'Here it is. Gopal Kutty. Only one name.'

'Is there an address?'

'No, only Mumbai.'

'Thank you. You've been most helpful,' Samir flashed his most polite smile and the children trooped out of the wooden office.

Gopal Kutty! They felt triumphant, as they headed back to Malabar village.

'That wasn't bad, was it?' Samir glanced at the others.

'It was ingeniously simple,' Tina chuckled, fiddling with her two pigtails.

'And now what do you plan to do with the name? Gopal Kutty…' Paras asked.

'Store it in my memory,' Samir grinned.

'Hello there!' a sweet voice called out to them and the children whirled around in surprise.

Mrs Fernando was walking down the hill from the direction of the huts, a large book clutched in her hands and a broad smile on her face.

'Hello, children! Isn't this cove simply adorable? I walked right up to this cove yesterday and loved it so much, that I decided I had to come again today.'

'It *is* a beautiful place,' Tina agreed, conversationally. 'Are you going to write about it in your book?'

'Yes, perhaps I will, it will make a praiseworthy scene—what with these quaint-looking huts, and coconut trees and the boats lapping gently in the blue water…' For a moment Mrs Fernando stared dreamily at the landscape around her and the book fell from her hands.

Tina bent down and picked it up, dusting the sand off. The writer took it from her hastily, thanking her and dusting the book again, as if Tina hadn't done a good enough job. Then she resumed her conversation, pleasantly talking about her past books.

'Are you walking back to the cottage? Good, I'll join you. I love kids. They are always so refreshing and when I am in the mood for writing something different—I mean apart from nature writing—they give me such wonderful ideas! I have many kid friends at home…' she rambled on.

'That saves us from a third children-hater. What with Jain and Sagar both competing for the children-hater position,' Samir muttered to Paras under his breath.

They were strolling past the long stretch of the beach. The sun was overhead again, with the clouds almost melting away. Mrs Fernando offered each one of them an éclair, which they accepted. Tina stopped to tie her shoe lace. The others walked on but Fulki waited for her cousin. She seemed to be taking an unnecessarily long time with her shoe.

'What's up?' Fulki asked, impatiently.

Tina gave her a smile and making sure that the others were out of ear-shot, said swiftly, 'It's Fernando's book. When I picked it up—it was as light as a feather! Can you imagine such a large and thick book to be so light?'

'Are you sure?'

'Positive,' Tina remarked, as they slowly followed the others.

'Perhaps it's made out of some special paper—I don't know…' Fulki frowned.

Tina shrugged. 'Possible but queer. You know, I've been thinking of all that we've seen till now—Jain's pistol, his unfriendliness, that note in our bedroom—it all seems *so* disconnected and *yet*

I have *this feeling* that it is all linked. Even those two men, who almost ran us off the road—I know it seems totally disjointed, but I can't help feeling that there is something serious in what we've seen so far. But then I wonder am I simply *overreacting*? You know, being highly imaginative?'

'To tell you the truth, nothing untoward has happened as yet. Of course, except for the note. But that could merely have been placed by either Jain or Sagar because they don't want to have children disturbing them here. Apart from that, the world is perfectly normal.'

'You're right—which means I *am* overreacting. So, let's just forget these unfriendly people and continue with our holidays, right? Because nothing has happened and nothing is *going* to happen!' Tina grinned, sheepishly.

'Right!' Fulki hugged her cousin and the two made their way after the others.

But things were about to happen and sooner than even Tina could have imagined!

SELL US YOUR PROJECT AND WE SHALL PAY YOU TEN TIMES MORE THAN WHAT YOUR GOVERNMENT WILL PAY YOU. PLACE A RED LIGHT ON YOUR WINDOW AT NIGHT AND WE SHALL KNOW YOU ARE INTERESTED.

8

A Letter and Night Disturbances

The children collected their bag of groceries from Panna's mother and lugged it up the hill. A volley of joyful barks greeted them at the door and Ruffy flung himself on them, licking their hands and faces. But the moment he saw Mrs Fernando, Ruffy's barks turned into deep, warning growls. Vijju immediately placed a hand over his collar and led him into the kitchen. The children handed the groceries over to Panna, who thanked them with hot bhajis.

Lunch was a quiet affair with both Sagar and Jain ordering their meals in their rooms. Only Fernando joined them but for once she seemed preoccupied. After a hearty lunch, the children for a change decided to take a nap. The long walk had tired them and the meal had turned them drowsy. They returned to their beds and within minutes, silence reigned in their rooms.

In the evening, the four of them walked around the cliff edge, enjoying the glorious sunset. Fulki sat down cross-legged on the flat rock and closed her eyes in meditation. The others left her in peace. After a while, she dug into her pocket and removed the crystal, cradling it gently in her palm and staring deeply into it.

'Find anything?' Samir teased and Tina frowned at him.

'Yes,' Fulki said in her strange voice. 'Tomorrow. Tomorrow is the day…note, more notes, something is going to happen…need to be careful…gun shots….'

She paused and even Samir kept silent, waiting for her to continue. But she did not. Instead she glanced up at the others.

'Do you believe me?'

'I do!' Tina supported, staunchly.

'I don't.' Samir grinned. 'And you have twenty-four hours to prove me wrong. Though, I must add, that you do a good job of it. You could turn this into a profession you know. With your curls, you could pass off as a gypsy any day.'

Fulki grinned. 'Thanks, I shall take that as a compliment.'

As the sun set, the children went back to the cottage. The rest of the evening passed rather well. They lazed around in the sitting-room and played a game of 'Challenge' with Vijju and Panna, who joined in for a change. Paras fetched the ladder from the kitchen and explored the book shelf. Finally, he sat down on the carpet, going through a heap of books. Ruffy went around demanding attention and getting patted affectionately by everyone. After an early dinner, the children began yawning again and one by one trooped off to bed. In spite of their afternoon nap, sleep swept over them like a soothing wave.

It was the next morning, after breakfast, that things started happening. The children had clattered down to the dining room, feeling refreshed and hungry, and had helped themselves to large helpings of *upma*. They were on their second helping, when Mr Sagar stormed into the room. He looked as if he was about to burst.

'Panna! Who's been here?' he thundered.

'No one of course! Why do you ask?' Panna was confused.

'Somebody has definitely been here. Read this. I found it under my door.' Sagar brandished a slip of paper, under her nose. 'Not only was someone here, but that someone also *knows* what I am working on.'

Panna took the piece of paper from him, muttering, 'Well, the milkman was here and the postman…' Then her eyes grew wide in shock.

Samir peered over Panna's shoulder and read the words aloud. 'SELL US YOUR PROJECT AND WE SHALL PAY YOU TEN TIMES MORE THAN WHAT YOUR GOVERNMENT WILL PAY YOU. PLACE A RED LIGHT ON YOUR WINDOW AT NIGHT AND WE SHALL KNOW YOU ARE INTERESTED.'

'Where did you find this?' Panna appeared dazed.

One by one, the children read the note, passing it forward. Samir frowned at Fulki. Had she gone this far to prove that her predictions could come true? It was a poor prank to play on Sagar. Tina was gazing at her cousin with open admiration. Fulki was amazing! But Fulki, on the contrary, looked stunned.

'I told you it was under my door. Have you mentioned, to anyone at all, in the village that I am here?' Sagar insisted.

'No, Sir.' Panna looked hurt. 'I wouldn't! I'm aware that your work is of utmost importance and I understand that perfectly. That you should suggest something....'

'Okay, I didn't mean it that way,' Sagar brushed away her indignance impatiently. 'But it is obvious that someone is very much aware of my whereabouts and my new project. What cheek, making me such an offer! Bribing me! Asking me to betray my country! If I ever catch the fellow, I'll teach him the lesson of a lifetime.' Sagar stomped angrily out of the dining room and banged straight into Fernando, who was just entering the room. He glared at her as if she was some species from outer space and strode out.

'What's the matter with *him*?' Fernando asked in surprise.

Just then Jain arrived as well and Panna related the event to them. Fernando's eyes widened in astonishment as she read the letter and shaking her head with disbelief, passed the note to Jain. The tall man read the note, his face expressionless. Tina nudged Fulki. He was in his tracksuit and the bulge in his back pocket showed prominently.

'This note sounds dangerous!' Fernando exclaimed. 'What is Mr Sagar planning to do?'

'Ignore it, of course,' Panna remarked, scornfully. 'He would never succumb to such demands. The true patriot that he is. . . .'

'Are you sure about that?' Jain spoke up for the first time, his eyes narrow.

'What do you mean?' Panna asked, the colour in her face rising.

'I mean that even the best of people give in to temptation. Mr Sagar would be no exception,' he drawled.

'Sagar*ji* is different. And I hope he never hears you talk like that. It would insult him and hurt him deeply.' Panna was clearly rattled.

'I was merely stating a fact, not accusing the esteemed Mr Sagar.' Jain shrugged and drawing out a chair, he sat down to eat his breakfast.

The children glanced at each other. Jain had reacted so strangely. What funny insinuations? What did he mean?

The cousins went out in the garden and sat down under the tree. The moment they were alone, Samir rounded on Fulki.

'You planted that note in Sagar*ji*'s room, didn't you? You had it all planned yesterday.'

'You're mad! Why would I do something like that?' Fulki retorted, angrily.

'Just to prove your predictions right, of course! All that crap about more notes and stuff, I can't believe this.'

'I can't believe you're accusing *me* of something so stupid and…and dangerous!' Fulki spluttered in anger. 'You're crazy if you think I would do something so crazy, just to prove my crystal right.'

'She's right, Samir. You're being most unfair. Fulki wouldn't do anything so stupid,' Paras said.

'You're just upset because her predictions *did* actually come true *again*. And that her crystal is really working,' Tina remarked, calmly. 'And now you two stop your bickering for once and let's *think*—I mean *really think*. What *exactly* is happening here?'

Samir nodded, grudgingly. 'I guess you're right. I'm sorry Fulki—I guess I just got carried away.' He grinned rather sheepishly.

'I'll accept your apology,' she replied, airily. 'For *everything* you've said so far!' She flashed him a smile.

'Good, now let's get down to business. Any ideas?' Tina spoke, briskly.

'I feel no outsider could have got into the house to slip in that note because Ruffy would have surely barked the place down and Panna would have noticed,' Paras commented.

'I strongly suspect Jain of being behind all this,' Samir remarked. 'He's got computer access and ever since we've seen him, he's behaved most oddly. Carrying that pistol around....'

'That could be for his own protection,' Fulki objected. 'It's not as if he has threatened anyone with his pistol, has he? Personally, I think he is okay.'

'You're only saying that because he's so handsome,' Samir scoffed. 'But, even you cannot deny that he *is* rather suspicious in his behaviour. Don't forget that he was observing the cottage through his binoculars.'

'Yes, but to be honest, we are merely *speculating*. We don't know anything for sure. We have no concrete proof that he is a villain, you know,' Paras said.

'Then who could have placed that note under Sagar*ji*'s door and who are these people who are trying to buy his project?' Tina wondered.

'It's all rather mysterious, isn't it?' Fulki said, fingering the crystal in her pocket. She dared not take it out. Already her two predictions were sending a chill down her back. 'I wonder what will happen tonight. Someone will be looking out and waiting for a signal in Sagar*ji*'s window. And, if he doesn't see it, then what? What will happen if Sagar*ji* disobeys them?'

None of the children had an answer to that question.

The rest of the day passed slowly, discussing and chatting. The clouds hung low over a dull and stuffy day. The children remained indoors and retired early for the night. They sat in the girls' bedroom with cups of hot chocolate before turning in.

'Do you think the person who wrote our note and Sagar*ji*'s note is one and the same?' Fulki asked.

'Difficult to say. Computer print-outs sometimes look so similar,' Samir replied. 'Unless of course, my hunch is right and it is Jain who has written those notes.'

'I say, come here at once!' Tina, who was standing near the window, spoke in an urgent voice.

The others immediately joined her at the window.

'What is it?'

'Can you see that red glow? From the direction of the island? It's quite far away though. Look! There it is again.' Tina pointed out a faint red flickering light in the great distant.

They watched as a light appeared, blinking in the dark and then vanished, repeating it's blinking at varying speed. As if it was deliberately trying to attract attention.

'That definitely looks as if it is shining from the direction of the island. Which means it has to be from the tower, only then can it be seen on the mainland,' Tina said.

'Possible. It does seem as if someone is signalling, doesn't it? Hey look, can you see a man down there?' Samir's voice had turned to a whisper.

They all strained their eyes. Sure enough, a dark figure was passing by, right under their window. They could hear the crunching of his feet on the gravel, as he made his way down to the cove and then vanished.

'Who could it be? Someone from the cottage? At this time of the night?' Tina stared at the others.

'A passer-by,' Paras suggested, a little doubtfully.

'Or someone answering that signal,' Tina said. 'Someone who is staying at the cottage.'

'But there are only two men here. Jain and Sagar*ji*...' Fulki's voice trailed off as she looked at the others, the startling thought in all their minds.

'*Sagarji*? But...would he, after the way he reacted this morning?' Paras asked.

'Well, stranger things have happened. Remember what Jain said in the morning? Temptation—it's a bad word sometimes,' Tina reminded.

'Let's not jump to any conclusions,' Samir interrupted, practically. 'That man need not have been from the cottage. He could have been just anyone around here—perhaps from the village. It was too dark to figure out anyway. For the time being, let's just keep quiet and keep our ears and eyes open, okay?'

Before anyone could respond, a distinct whirr of a motorboat reached their ears.

'A motorboat! Heading away from mainland at this time of the night? There wasn't any boat in the cove this evening, was there?' Tina frowned.

'How do we know? We didn't go to the cove at all today. It may or may not have been there,' Fulki reminded.

'It's got to be that man who left in the boat. And I shall bet that he's heading towards the island,' Samir said, confidently. 'This gets more and more intriguing. What *is* happening here?'

'I've an idea! Let's wait for a while and see if that man returns. If he is from the cottage, he'll definitely come up this way. Then we'll know for sure whether he's our scientist or not,' Paras suggested.

The others agreed and they sat chatting for half an hour. But suddenly a heavy downpour began and absolutely nothing could be seen or heard over the black roar of the falling rain. Finally, the children gave up. It was useless to keep vigil when vision was impossible.

'I've a better idea,' Tina said. 'The motorboat will be parked in the cove, if at all it returns tonight. We can go and check it up first thing in the morning.'

'And then we can go to Ranpar and find out the name of the person who hired it too,' Fulki agreed, her eyes gleaming.

'Good idea! In any case, I couldn't have stayed awake a moment longer,' Paras yawned loudly and that set the rest of them yawning.

The boys went to their room and silence reigned as soon as their heads touched the pillows. They slept so soundly that they did not hear the motorboat return, the cottage door open and someone creep into the bed.

The next morning the weather was still cloudy. But the coolness in the air was refreshing and welcome after the heat of the day before. Immediately after breakfast, the children ran down to the cove and sure enough, a motorboat lapped gently on the water.

'Why, it's the same boat Gopal Kutty hired!' Paras exclaimed, staring at the multicoloured boat.

'Does that mean that Gopal is around or someone else has hired the same boat?' Fulki wondered.

'The only way to find out is to go to Ranpar and chat with that man again.' Samir grinned.

'And what will you tell him this time?' Tina laughed.

'The truth, I think. Though, I can't guarantee results this time. Let's go and find out, all the same.'

They enjoyed the walk down the beach. Vijju and Ruffy joined them. The Desai children related the night's events to Vijju and his eyes opened in astonishment.

'Now I understand why Ruffy was growling last night. I did hear a rustling and I thought he'd seen a mouse. So, it was a man going down to the cove,' he said.

They reached Ranpar village and walked to the cove nestled between the cliffs. The boats stood in a riot of colour but the wooden office was empty. The children hung around for a while but the man in charge did not turn up. Finally, the children began to get restless.

'What now?' Tina sighed.

'The register is on the table. Why don't we just take a peek in it? I'm sure it won't do any harm,'

Samir suggested, his eyes shining. 'Just stay on guard outside while I pop in and take a look, okay?'

The others agreed and the girls immediately took their place outside the office with Vijju and Ruffy. The boys quickly stepped inside the shack and thumped through the pages of the register. There it was, the same name again! Gopal Kutty! In a matter of minutes, Samir and Paras were out. Briskly all of them walked away from the office and went down towards the beach.

'If that boat was hired by Gopal Kutty, what does it mean?' Vijju frowned in concentration.

'It means that Gopal Kutty is around somewhere, using that boat in the dead of night—apparently to meet his friend on the island. Though why he should travel at night is a great mystery.'

'But how is it connected with us? I mean with Sagar*ji*, and who was the man who walked towards the cove last night?' Vijju persisted.

'I wish we knew,' Tina said, wistfully. 'It really is all very confusing. We don't even know who Gopal is and if there is any connection between him and what we saw last night.'

'And what roles do Sagar*ji* and Jain have to play in all this,' Paras reminded with a resigned sigh.

Ruffy suddenly woofed at them, jumping around and snapping at their heels.

'Yes, I can do with some game too, Ruffy! I'm quite tired of trying to answer questions that I cannot answer.' Samir laughed. 'Come on, race me to that point!' And with that, Samir set off across the beach with Ruffy at his heels.

Soon the others joined in the game and the atmosphere lightened at once. The children raced and jumped over the waves and for an hour forgot all about the mysteries of the cottage. Finally, around lunch time, they returned to the cottage, their stomachs growling and all set to do justice to Panna's excellent preparations.

9 Finally, The Tunnel!

The following couple of days passed uneventfully. There were no more light signals, or notes, and the motorboat stood in the cove unattended.

The children spent their time helping Vijju search for the tunnel. They covered every inch of the cliff and went through some of the caves again, but there was no sign of the tunnel.

'This is too bad. We've searched high and low and in all possible places for the tunnel. And now I have this horrible feeling that the tunnel doesn't exist at all,' Samir said in a despairing tone. He flopped down on a rock and mopped his perspiring face with a hanky.

'I hope that isn't true,' Fulki said. 'Not after the way we have been hunting for it. It just wouldn't be fair!'

'The tunnel exists. I know it exists,' Vijju insisted in a low fierce voice.

'If it does, it is high time it showed up,' Paras remarked.

'You know, I think we are going about this search in a most unmethodical manner,' Tina spoke up with sudden insight.

'Really?' Paras raised a mocking eyebrow.

'If I had to make a tunnel—a secret tunnel without anybody's knowledge, where would I build it? In a place away from prying eyes certainly, and somewhere I can work in peace without being disturbed,' she explained, patiently. 'And where would such a place be?'

'My home?' Samir supplied.

'Exactly! The cottage. We've searched everywhere but the cottage.'

'Of course!' Vijju exclaimed. 'Why didn't I ever think of it? The tunnel must be somewhere in the cottage.'

'Come on, let's go in and start at once.' Fulki jumped up enthusiastically and the others caught her excitement. Ruffy barked, appreciatively.

They began walking back to the cottage, almost running and tripping over Ruffy in their haste.

'But, where do we begin? I mean the tunnel could be anywhere in the cottage—perhaps even in Sagar*ji*'s or Jain's room,' Vijju realised in dismay. 'And *Aai* will never allow us to enter those rooms.'

'I've been thinking,' Tina replied. 'You have so many books in the house—some very old and on the history of this area. Perhaps there may be a mention of the cottage and the secret tunnel?'

Vijju's eyes lit up. 'Great idea! I've seen many books where the cottage is mentioned, though I haven't touched them in ages. But I never thought of checking out the tunnel. I'll get the ladder immediately.'

As soon as they entered the cottage, Vijju ran to collect the ladder from the kitchen. In the meanwhile, the children began going through the books on the lower shelves.

'Here's one—*Malabar Village, A History*,' Samir said, quickly going through the index.

'And I've found one too,' Paras said. '*The Story of Malabar*.'

The children discovered several books, scanning through the pages, but they could find no reference to the cottage or the tunnel. When Vijju returned with the ladder, Paras shinned up and searched the top shelves. He dropped some books down to the others, his fingers covered with a thick layer of dust. Samir picked up *Malabar: Then and Now*, and Tina opened *The History of Malabar Island*.

'Hey! Here's a reference to the cottage in *Malabar—Unravelled*! And the secret rooms...the passage in our room,' Fulki exclaimed.

'But what about the tunnel?' Samir asked, impatiently.

Fulki was silent as she quickly read on. 'Yes, it's here! Come on down, Paras, I think we've found it!' she shouted.

The children gathered over the book as she read about the secret tunnel, which took about fifteen minutes to reach the island.

'And there's a map here and some indications. Vijju, do you think you can identify these marks?'

Fulki handed the book to the boy and he took it eagerly. For a moment, he stared at the page and the others waited with bated breath. At last, he looked up and his eyes were shining brilliantly.

'We've found it!' he cried, triumphantly. 'It's right here, in the sitting room, in the....'

'The secret room,' Tina guessed.

'Right under our noses!' Fulki gasped.

'Are you sure this is not a false lead?' Samir asked, on a sudden note of pessimism and the others promptly objected to this idea.

'Why not find out immediately? Fernando and Jain are both out and Sagar*ji* is in his room,' Vijju suggested and an affirmative chorus rang out.

Vijju headed to the lamp and turned the lamp to the right. The panel slowly glided aside.

'Finally! On the verge of discovery,' Paras whispered.

'Since all of us won't fit in, let's take turns searching,' Vijju said.

Samir and Vijju stepped in first and began tapping and knocking all over the small room. The others stood outside and watched eagerly, as the two boys went over the walls one by one. Ruffy put up his paws on the edge and pushed his big head in, equally curious.

'There's nothing here,' came Samir's disappointed voice.

'Come out and let us take our turn,' Fulki said.

They exchanged places. The girls tapped and tugged and pulled till their hands felt bruised but to no avail. Paras also joined them.

'There's a niche here! Right on the top!' he remarked, as his fingers touched the tiny crevice.

The children crowded around him at once and Ruffy, sensing their excitement, began to bark.

'Do you think it is the opening to the tunnel?' Samir asked.

Vijju placed his hand inside the niche, which was hidden near the ceiling and felt along the line. Suddenly, a loud grating sound filled the tight-packed little room, making the children jump.

They watched in fascination as the back of the room rumbled and slowly slid away, sounding like a low grumble at being disturbed after years! A cold, damp wave rushed toward them, making them shiver.

'At last!' Vijju said, his eyes shining happily. '*Ajji* will be delighted!'

Samir put his head into the yawning hole and turned his torch on. He could see rough steps vanishing into the darkness. When he spoke his voice sounded hollow and booming. 'I think these steps are going straight underground, perhaps under the sea.'

'What do you say? Should we try the tunnel out?' Tina grinned at others.

There was no need to ask. They were all too eager to step in.

'We'll need more torches. We don't want to get lost under the sea,' Samir said.

Ruffy did not seem to understand what was happening. He swished his tail, trying to climb down.

'No Ruffy, you have to stay here on guard, okay? I shall whistle if I need you,' Vijju told him solemnly.

Tina laughed. 'He won't be able to hear your whistle, silly. We shall be far away on the island!'

Samir and Paras fetched the torches and soon the children were ready to set off. Ruffy watched, a little unhappily, as one by one, the children stepped into the black hole and vanished.

The tunnel was narrow in the beginning but as they descended cautiously, it began to broaden. After a little while, the steps gave way to a sandy, even path.

'We are under the hill, or rather inside it,' Samir spoke in a muffled voice. He was in the lead and his torch cut a neat, illuminated path through the dark.

'I can't believe that we've actually found the tunnel and are going through it,' Vijju said in awe and the others smiled.

'Your dream of years has come true,' Fulki said. 'I say, what's that sound?'

A low, steady booming sound seemed to come right from overhead, filling the tunnel. It seemed to echo like a murmur through the tunnel and as they walked on, it became distinctly louder.

'That's the sea,' Vijju explained. 'We are under the sea. I think the roof has weakened in places and that is why the sound seems to grow louder.'

'You mean the roof can fall in any moment?' Fulki asked, alarmed. She stopped in her tracks and Paras who was following her, bumped into her.

'Ouch!' he hung on to his glasses which had almost tipped off.

'No, the roof won't fall in, at least not at the moment. Erosion is a slow and steady process which takes years,' Samir told his sister. 'Doesn't your crystal tell you that?'

'Samir!' Tina warned.

'Let him, Tina, it's his way of showing how unsporting he is!' Fulki spoke airily.

Samir stopped suddenly and once again they all bumped into each other. Paras saved his glasses just in time. Samir ignored their groans. 'There's a bifurcation here. I don't know which route to take.'

The tunnel divided into two and the children gathered at the fork, wondering what to do.

'I vote we try both the ways. Two of us can take the left route and the others can take the right one. See you back in five minutes,' Paras suggested.

The others agreed. Vijju and Paras took the left turning. The tunnel seemed to go deeper down into the sea and a few minutes later, they returned to the fork. Samir and the girls were waiting for them.

'We reached a dead-end,' Fulki informed.

'Right. Ours went straight on,' Vijju replied.

Once again they were on their way. The floor was even and sandy and it seemed as if they had walked for ages before they saw another opening.

'The tunnel ends here,' Samir said, puzzled. A stone wall stood in the centre of the tunnel and they all wondered if the roof had fallen in.

'Look, there's another hole on this side of the wall,' Vijju observed. It was a much smaller hole, totally hidden in the dark.

The children had to bend low, as they entered another tunnel which began rising steeply. The sandy floor made their feet slip and the children had to sometimes move on all fours. The air was musty and damp and breathing was laborious.

'This is steep. We'll have a problem climbing down again,' Tina said.

'I think we are finally at our destination!' Samir's voice was filled with excitement. 'There's a rung ladder here. It might lead straight to the castle!'

He began climbing carefully, checking each rung before stepping on it. The others followed slowly, wondering where it would lead. They emerged out of a small hole into a large, cold room. Huge rusted, iron rings were attached to the wall.

'The famous dungeon!' Paras whispered.

'Yes, see those big rings? People were tied to those rings and left to die.'

The children were silent as they looked at the room. A feeling of death still clung to the old, cold walls, giving the room an evil air.

'Let's get out of here,' Fulki suggested in a small voice and the others agreed.

Steps led out into another passage and as they climbed out, they heaved a sigh of relief. They were in the courtyard and they ran into the sunshine.

'Whew! I have never valued sunshine more than I do now.' Fulki laughed.

They all felt the same. The sun really felt wonderful after the dark mustiness and the island looked more picturesque than ever. The children flopped down on the grass and breathed in lungfuls of the fresh sea air.

'I feel drained out with all this excitement,' Vijju sighed. But he looked most relaxed and contented.

'While we are here, why don't we check out if anyone is living in the tower?' Tina asked, with a gleam in her eyes.

'Yes, let's,' Samir agreed, getting up at once.

They had to pull Fulki up, who groaned but allowed herself to be dragged. They went up the narrow spiral staircase, carefully avoiding looking down. Once on the top, Samir tried the door.

'It's locked.'

'Which means someone *is* living here. It wasn't locked the last time we came. So it's got to be one of the two men.' Tina deducted.

'And that means they could have given the light signal the other night,' Paras added, as they made their way down the staircase again.

Since it was past lunch time, they hastened back to the dungeons. The journey back was easier, since they knew the way. The tunnel did not seem so long either. Ruffy met them with loud, joyful barks as they stepped out of the room.

The rest of the day was spent discussing about the tunnel and the children decided to let Panna into the secret. She was thrilled to hear about their success and wanted to see it immediately. Vijju showed it to her and her face glowed with satisfaction.

In the evening, Panna's mother also got the news. Her face beamed with happiness. She hugged Vijju and Ruffy. 'Wonderful! You children cannot imagine what an important discovery it is!' she exclaimed.

'It was sheer luck actually,' Paras said, honestly.

'That doesn't belittle what you did. You deserve an ice-cream each.'

The children chatted with Panna's mother for a while as they devoured their gifts.

'I'll be there to see the tunnel as soon as I can. Wild horses can't keep me away from exploring it,' she declared and they all laughed.

It was with a great deal of satisfaction and a feeling of well-being that the children returned to the cottage.

10

Gunshots and the Tunnel Again

'PLACE THE PAPERS IN THE MOTORBOAT AT MIDNIGHT, IF YOU WANT TO LIVE.'

The children stared at the printed words, as Sagar*ji* hopped with rage. They were in the dining room eating lunch and the scientist had come down with the note.

'Threatening *me*...I can't believe it!' Mr Sagar exclaimed, his face beet red.

Jain, who was eating silently at the table, stood up and took the note from Samir, two worry lines etched deeply in his forehead.

'What are you going to do about it?' he asked, casually.

'Do about it? Ignore it, of course!' Mr Sagar replied, scornfully. 'Whoever these people are, they are not going to frighten me. And they will never get away with it. I shall see to it...I....'

To the children's surprise, Jain took Sagar's hand and murmuring something under his breath, led him out of the room. The children glanced at each other. What did it mean? Jain was telling the scientist something in undertones and he actually seemed to be listening. Or had the industrialist been trying to stop Sagar from saying...too much? A startling idea invaded Tina's thoughts. Were the two men *friends*?

'What do you think Sagar*ji* plans to do?' Vijju looked worried.

The children were sitting out in the garden, eating mangoes.

'His reaction was obvious, wasn't it? I'm sure he will not co-operate,' Samir said.

'But these people mean business. They could harm him or something,' Vijju said, alarmed.

'What really concerns me is who writes these notes and how do they get into Sagar*ji*'s room,' Fulki wondered.

'I was just wondering...did you see how Jain and Sagar*ji* talked in low voices? I found it most surprising. Somehow, the idea that Sagar*ji* is not completely innocent is really growing in my mind,' Tina said, thoughtfully.

'No, I can't believe that,' Paras protested. 'He's a man of great repute—you yourself once said that. And somehow, I don't think he could have faked his reactions to those notes. He seemed so *genuine!'*

'It's just a thought.' Tina shrugged. 'I'm not accusing him of anything. I simply felt curious the way Jain spoke to him.'

'In any case, tonight we can keep watch and find out what happens,' Samir said. 'I have a gut feeling that tonight we shall have the answers to some of our questions.'

'I'm glad someone is optimistic here.' Tina grinned.

But that night, all of them were tense. Dinner had been a quiet affair. Jain and Sagar ate their meal in silence. Even the children were hushed, as if something had already happened. Only Fernando, who had been out the whole day and was unaware of the note, chatted with Panna, who replied in monosyllables.

Later, the children sat reading in the girls' room. Vijju and Ruffy joined them. It was a stuffy, moonless night and the sky was ink black with thick clouds. It was going to rain again. A perfect night for dark dealings.

'I can't read any more. I'm too restless. I wish it would be midnight soon,' Samir said, finally dropping his book on the table.

'Me too.' Tina agreed.

Paras, who was standing guard at the window, yawned. 'And I'm feeling too sleepy to care. This really isn't any of our concern....'

The others came down on him heavily.

'What do you mean? This is serious!'

'How can you speak like that?'

'This is a mystery just like in the books, and we are investigating like we always dreamed of.'

'Don't you feel responsible?'

Ruffy barked.

'Okay, okay.' Paras laughed, raising a hand in defence. 'I was just joking.'

He turned to the window again and just in time spotted a dark figure slipping past their window. He immediately gestured to the others, motioning them to the spot. The others hastened to his side. Sure enough, a tall man was making his way carefully down the path.

'It *is* Sagar*ji*!' Fulki whispered, in a shocked voice.

'Which means he's succumbing to their demands,' Tina said. 'But it's not yet midnight.'

'Perhaps he wanted to get done with it. Should we follow him or wait for him to return?'

'He's only supposed to keep his papers in the boat. Let's wait for him to return. Besides, we don't know if he really *is* the victim,' Tina suggested.

'But suppose he's innocent and doesn't return? Suppose they are waiting for him down there and they kidnap him?' Paras asked.

The others were quiet, thinking. It was true that they didn't know anything for certain. It was all so confusing. But if Sagar*ji* had nothing to do with these people, then he *could* be in danger.

'I think we should go down there. Just Paras and me. You girls wait here,' Samir said.

'I'm coming too,' Vijju insisted. 'But, what about Ruffy?'

'He may bark and create problems. In any case, we are just keeping an eye on Sagar*ji*,' Paras said. 'We'll be back soon.'

So, a disgruntled Ruffy stayed with the girls. The boys took their torches and slipped out of the main door. The girls watched from the window and waved, as they crept down the hill. It was quite impossible to see in the dark and soon the three figures vanished from sight. The girls waited with bated breath. Ten minutes passed and then twenty.

'Look, there's Sagar*ji* returning. But where are the boys?' Fulki wondered, puzzled.

Half an hour passed and they began to get worried. It was a quarter past midnight.

Suddenly, a shot rang out in the dark and Tina and Fulki looked at each other, shocked. What was happening? Why were their brothers and Vijju not back yet? Ruffy whined. The suspense was driving all of them mad!

'Should we go down? I'm worried,' Fulki asked.

'I don't know. We may complicate matters, if we do. We don't know what's happening down there. Let's wait for ten more minutes and then decide what to do,' Tina replied, looking equally frustrated.

Just then they heard the whirr of a motorboat. Someone was heading out toward the island!

'I can't wait anymore! Let's go down there.' Fulki and Tina spoke together, and Ruffy barked in agreement.

They grabbed the torches, put on their rain jackets and shoes, and slipped out of their room. They went down the stairs and to the main door which was shut. They opened it quietly and stepped out into the warm night. They circled the cottage and set off down the tricky path. Their torches shone on the rocks which winked as if the stones had sequins on them. The two girls stumbled along, fervently praying that all was well with the boys. There was still no sign of them. Ruffy ran on ahead, knowing exactly where and why they were going. At last they arrived at the cove. The night was silent and the cove looked sinister and deserted. Samir, Paras and Vijju were nowhere to be seen and the boat was missing too. Ruffy began sniffing at once. Suddenly, he ran into a corner and barked. The girls ran to where he was standing over a dark form.

'Someone is lying here! Could it be....' Tina turned the huddled figure over as she spoke and her breath caught in her throat

'Jain!' Fulki exclaimed, horrified. She knelt beside Tina to help her. 'Blood! He's...he's been shot!'

'He's alive, the wound is in the arm, I think,' Tina informed her after checking for signs of breathing.

Just then Jain groaned and moved. His eyes flickered open and he stared at the two girls in the torch light. His eyes grew wide as he recognised them, recalling what had transpired and struggled to sit up.

'There's a hanky in my pocket,' he whispered. 'Take it and tie up my....'

Tina hesitated, but realising the consequences of blood loss, hastened to follow instructions.

'Thank you,' he said, simply.

'What happened?' Fulki asked. 'Where are the boys?'

'That man took them away in the boat. I don't know where. If I hadn't got this gun-shot in my arm and fainted, I would have prevented it from happening.' He sighed.

The girls looked at each other. So Jain was trying to help. But why and what was he doing here?

'We know where they've gone. To the island,' Tina guessed. 'But what exactly happened? I mean here. Why did he shoot at you when you had a pistol....'

'Oh, you know about it, do you?' Jain gave a weak smile. 'I thought you kids were smart. But I think it's time to explain. I'm a CBI Officer!'

The girls gasped! Police! And they had thought he was a criminal.

'I was sent on special duty to the cottage since we knew Sagar was working on his new project. Security measures...in disguise. We had an idea that someone would be after him.'

'Oh, that's why you've been scouting through binoculars and carrying a pistol around,' Fulki said.

'Yes. When the second note arrived this morning, Sagar and I made a plan. We decided to pretend to obey orders so that I could catch them red-handed. And I almost did. But I got shot. Then the boys who were hiding until then, ran to help me and even tried to stop the man from leaving in the motorboat. Unfortunately, another man appeared from the dark and together they out-powered the children. Then I fainted. And you found me here.'

'And now, we must find the boys. They could be in danger!' Tina stood up, helping Jain get up.

'And you need to get to a doctor too,' Fulki added.

'Oh no! First, we have to reach the boys and *you two* don't have to do anything. It's time for me to call in the police. We need help,' Jain said, firmly.

'But it may be too late, till then!' Fulki cried.

'There's no other way. How can you reach the island, without a boat, in the middle of the night?'

'We can, through the tunnel!'

Jain listened intently as the two girls explained about the tunnel which ran right up to the castle. The amazed expression on his face pleased the girls.

'I will, of course, come along,' the Officer said.

'Oh, the tunnel is very low and narrow, Sir, you wouldn't be able to walk tall and certainly not with your injury. But we'll take Ruffy along this time,' Tina added, quickly.

'But...,' Jain began and stopped. The grim determination on their faces clearly told him that they were not willing to listen. He appeared doubtful as they climbed up to the cottage, slowly.

'Just be careful. In the meanwhile, I'll contact the police for help,' he said at length.

They reached the cottage and Fulki ran to her room. She removed the crystal from its box and the stone glinted in the light. She closed her palm over it and concentrated with all her heart.

'Come on, Fulki, hurry...,' Tina began, then stopped short.

Fulki was standing very still. Gradually, she opened her eyes and smiled at her cousin.

'I'm ready. Let's go!'

Minutes later, Jain watched in astonishment, as the panel glided open and the two girls climbed into the secret room, with Ruffy on a leash. Then, with a loud grating sound, the secret tunnel gaped open. A draft of cold air met them and they shivered.

'I wish I could go with you...it is too dangerous to let you girls go on your own.' He frowned.

'Don't worry, Sir. With Ruffy with us, we will be quite safe,' Fulki assured and Tina nodded her head vigorously.

'I guess, I don't have much of a choice, do I? And I do see your point about the tunnel being low and narrow. And the police will be here any minute too.' Jain gave a thumbs-up sign.

Fulki and Tina stepped into the tunnel and slowly descended the stairs following in the arrow-sharp torch light. Ruffy kept pulling at the leash, but Tina retained a strong hold on him. For a short while, they continued their journey in silence. Then the sound of the sea increased overhead.

'I hope those men have not hurt the boys,' Fulki said in a worried voice.

'Let's hope not, since they really have nothing to gain from them. They wanted Sagar*ji*'s project and perhaps they have it now. For all you know, they may have even vanished with the papers and released the boys, safe and sound, at the cottage,' Tina said, but she did not sound very convinced herself.

'I'm so glad Ruffy is with us. This tunnel seems really scary without the boys.'

'I'm glad he's with us too.'

They arrived at the tiny hole in the wall and squeezed through it. Ruffy followed lightly. Then the girls began the steep climb up the sandy slope. Ruffy kept slipping and any other time the girls would have laughed, but now they only urged the dog on.

'I say, we'll have to leave Ruffy behind in the tunnel. We can't take him up the ladder!' Fulki realised, suddenly.

'I hadn't thought of that either,' Tina said in dismay. 'I guess we have no choice. Ruffy, wait for us here, will you? And don't budge, okay?'

Ruffy whined, as if in protest. Tina sat down beside him and patted him gently. 'We are going to look for Vijju and we'll find him. Just stay here and don't go away.'

This time Ruffy barked. He watched with solemn eyes as the girls ascended the ladder.

'I wish we didn't have to leave Ruffy behind,' Fulki said, as they emerged into the dark dungeons. 'This is the most horrible part of the castle!'

They hurried out into the courtyard. Fortunately, the moon was out from behind the clouds, throwing a blue sheen over the stone courtyard.

'The Tower?' Fulki whispered and her cousin nodded.

That was the most likely place where the boys would be held prisoners. And if they were not there, then they would go down to the cove and check the motorboat. As quietly as possible, they began climbing the spiral staircase and finally reached the top. The tower door was shut but not locked.

'There's a latch. Should we go in?' Fulki wondered, but did not wait for an answer. They *had to* check if the boys were inside, regardless of anything else.

She slowly slid the latch away and it made a scratching sound which boomed in the night silence. The door pushed open and the girls stepped into the room bathed with moonlight.

'Tina! Fulki! How did you get here?' Samir exclaimed.

The boys were resting against the wall, their hands and legs tied. It took a few minutes for Fulki and Tina to explain, as they hastily untied the prisoners.

'And what about you? What happened?'

'We arrived just in time to see a scuffle going on between Jain and a man. Then he shot at Jain and we threw caution to the winds and ran to help. But suddenly another man sprang from behind us. I guess with a gun pointed at us, we couldn't do much, could we? But let's not talk now. We have to get out of here. The men have gone down for a few minutes, to discuss something. They were arguing loudly and didn't want us to hear,' Samir spoke in hushed whispers.

They all rushed down the way they had come. The girls were almost in a daze, now that they knew the boys were safe. They were crossing the courtyard, when they heard the shout.

'Hey you, stop!'

'Oh no! He's come and he's got a gun with him. Run to the dungeons!' Paras shouted.

The man was in hot pursuit, cursing loudly. His feet clattered on the courtyard. They reached the dungeons and Tina switched on the torches. One by one, the children rushed down the ladder, their hearts beating painfully. They could hear the man crossing the courtyard and entering the dungeons with loud, thumping footsteps. Samir was the last to climb down and as he stepped on the first rung, a hand caught him roughly by the scruff of his neck.

'Caught you, you little rat!' the man hissed. 'Thought you would get away from me, eh?'

Samir gritted his teeth. He made an effort to twist his head, but the man's grip was strong. Desperately, he struggled, his legs slipping from the rung and flailing. As the man tried to drag him up, Samir tried hard to keep a foothold on to the rungs.

He then started giving in to the man's pull which made the man a tad less alert for a few precious seconds. At that very moment, Samir gathered all his strength and pulled down making the man lose his balance. The sudden pull made him fall through the hole and down the ladder, dragging Samir with him. They both crumpled in a heap at the bottom of the ladder. The gun flew from his hand and dropped in a corner. Before the man could get up, Ruffy pounced on him, growling furiously.

'Good dog, Ruffy! Go on him!' ordered Vijju and Ruffy barred his teeth.

'Don't let that dog on me, please! Take him away!' the man begged but the dog ignored his pleas and snapped at his feet.

Samir picked up the gun carefully and levelled it at the man.

'Okay, get back and start walking. You first. If you act smart, not only will I shoot but the dog will tear you to pieces. Now walk!'

The others gazed at Samir with admiration. Hindi films sure had their positive effect on him. Fulki shivered, looking at the loaded gun, as the man stumbled and began walking after Vijju and Ruffy. Samir followed them and the rest of them fell in line.

The journey back was slow and cautious and Samir kept a sharp look on the man. But he was too frightened to take any risk. It seemed ages before they arrived at the stone steps leading to the secret room. Light shone from the top. They clambered out and were immediately met by Jain.

When Jain saw who had stepped out of the hole, he remarked, 'My, my. We have company.' But his face also registered shock.

Two constables were waiting in the sitting room and they immediately handcuffed the man. Panna had also been awoken by Jain, whose arm was now bandaged.

'What exactly is happening here?' she asked faintly, hugging her son and patting Ruffy.

'My papers! What about my papers?' Sagar*ji* appeared in sight. His hair was dishevelled and he seemed totally shaken by the night's happenings.

'Relax, Sagar*ji*, you know they were not the real papers,' Jain reminded and the scientist's face broke into a grin.

'Of course. I forgot we planted the fake formula!'

The children flopped down on the sofa, tired but satisfied and Panna pushed off to make hot chocolate for them.

'Well, you children are amazing!' Jain said. 'I would have never thought... Anyway, excellent work.'

The children grinned their thanks, feeling too tired all of a sudden to say much.

'The second man is still free, Sir. The man called Gopal Kutty. We heard the two men talking in the boat. After they tied us and left us in the tower, Gopal Kutty was going to return to the mainland.'

'Don't worry, we'll catch him. Now, you children drink your chocolate and have a good night's sleep—I mean whatever is left of the night. We'll talk tomorrow, okay?'

The children did not have the energy to argue. They quickly drank up the chocolate Panna brought them and trooped off to bed. Their heads had barely touched the pillows, when sleep enveloped them in a big, dreamless wave.

The Mystery is Solved

Mrs Fernando was amazed when she heard all the details of the night's events. She couldn't believe that she had slept through all the excitement. Over a late breakfast, the children told Jain all that they knew about the two men—how they had met them on the island and seen one of them stay back, about finding out the name Gopal Kutty, and how they had seen someone go to the cove one night.

'We also saw you carry your pistol and wondered what you had to do with this business,' Tina reported, evasively.

Jain grinned, looking very handsome indeed. 'You mean, you *suspected* me? Well, I can't blame you. I did my level best to be as unfriendly as possible. It was an effort to disguise myself—in dress as well as manner. I tried to be rude so that you kids would go away. I didn't want you in the midst of anything terrible happening here, as we guessed it would—what with Sagar*ji* working on this most secret formula.'

'You kept that note in our room, didn't you?' Fulki asked, a little shyly.

'Yes, it was the only way to warn you to leave. If I knew you would ignore the note, I wouldn't have bothered. And, of course, if I had *any idea,* that you would prove more useful than *me* in solving matters, I would have invited you to help me.' He laughed.

Panna came to clear the table and Mrs Fernando announced, 'I'm leaving today, Panna. Much as I like it here, I simply cannot work. Too much noise and excitement.'

'All the excitement is over. Nothing will disturb you now.' Samir grinned.

She shook her head. 'Even so, I cannot. I've got a writer's block and it won't go away, unless I change my location. Goodbye, in case I don't meet you again.' She smiled at them and left the table.

Panna shrugged. 'I cannot force anyone to stay, can I?'

The children continued to chat about their adventure with Jain. They were still getting the bits and pieces of the plot together. It was the tall man who had sent Mr Sagar the anonymous notes. A laptop and printer were discovered in the tower room. Though how those notes got under the scientist's door, was still a mystery.

'Maybe he really did enter the house when no one was around?' Paras guessed.

'Twice? Seems almost impossible.' Jain shook his head. 'Surely, he would be seen.'

'Earlier we thought that you had sent those notes. It was really a most convenient answer since you had a laptop and printer too,' Samir said.

'Yes, I really goofed up that part, didn't I? I really was a first-class suspect.' Jain laughed heartily again.

Ruffy barked, almost in agreement and that made Jain laugh louder. He patted the dog and dropped him some cake, which the dog gobbled up immediately. Panna too gave Ruffy a special treat for his brave performance the previous night. He truly deserved the biggest chicken leg piece!

The children were about to leave the breakfast table when Mr Sagar strode into the room. To their amazement, he looked upset.

'Has anyone been to my room?' he asked, a deep scowl on his face. 'My papers and a CD with the most important formula on it are missing.'

'But you haven't even left the room today,' Jain said.

'Of course, I did. I did take a bath and took loo breaks, didn't I?'

'Why would any one of us take anything from your room?' Panna asked, slightly irritated. 'You must have misplaced your things.'

'I'm not a fool to misplace the most important discovery of my life,' Sagar barked. 'Jain, you've got to do something about this.'

'Calm down. We'll get down to the bottom of this,' Jain spoke soothingly, as if talking to a small child.

'Could that bald man called Gopal have stolen the papers?' Paras wondered.

'How and when?' Fulki countered.

No one had an answer to that. The children speculated with Jain while Sagar frowned and chewed his lip in frustration.

Only Tina was quiet and her face held a strange expression, as if she was struck by something. Why hadn't she thought of it? Why hadn't she seen the truth?

Just then Mrs Fernando entered with her bag. 'Panna, should we settle our accounts?' Then, realising the tense atmosphere in the room, she glanced at the others. '*Now* what's the matter? I thought everything was over.'

'Someone has stolen Sagar*ji*'s papers and CD from his room,' Panna explained.

Mrs Fernando looked shocked. 'But, how is that possible? Who would dare enter the house and his room?'

'That's exactly what we intend to find out,' Tina remarked, slowly.

'Then please, excuse me. I have a bus to catch. Panna, shall we?' Fernando clutched her bag, ready to go.

'One moment, Mrs Fernando. Can you just hang on for a minute?' Tina asked, sweetly.

Too sweetly, the others noticed.

Tina turned to Jain and said, 'You're looking for Gopal Kutty, aren't you? Or whatever his real name is? And the person who has stolen Sagar*ji*'s papers and CD? Well, here is the man you want!'

To everyone's great astonishment, Tina moved swiftly towards Mrs Fernando and with a jerk, pulled at her hair. The hair came off and the square glasses tumbled to the floor, revealing a bald, shining head and frightened eyes!

A gasp followed this action and then a hushed silence, as the others took in the turn of events.

Fernando! Gopal Kutty? Jain instantly moved forward and clasped handcuffs on the man dressed as a woman. He then stared at Tina with his piercing eyes and asked, 'The papers and the CD?'

Tina smiled. 'It's in her…I mean, in *his* book. It is hollow inside and contains the CD and the papers!'

'Tina, you're a genius!' Paras exclaimed, pushing back his glasses. 'How did you ever guess that it was Fernando?'

They were all relaxing in the sitting room and Sagar*ji* was listening intently. Jain had taken Fernando into custody and left for the police station.

Tina laughed, pleased with herself and the turn of events. 'It was sheer luck actually. Somehow, it all just clicked into place. I remembered something she had said in her first meeting—about seeing the kites circling the tower, when she had gone for a walk. Even then, I had found it odd. How could she see the kites from the mainland? It was a strange remark. It meant that she had been to the castle, but did not want to reveal it to us.

We had met the two men on the island on the very day she had arrived. It struck me today that if she had arrived on the same day as we went to the island, then how did she see the kites? Unless, she was on the island the same day as she claimed to have seen the kites. This meant that she had to be one of the two men because there was no one else on the island!

'Then the other day, when her book fell down and I picked it up, it was amazingly light. Besides, she literally snatched it from my hand. I thought it was strange for a big book to be so light. But I did not give it much thought then. And then there was the business of the notes, the ease with which they were slipped under the door, without anyone seeing them.

Other things like—someone answering the signal and slipping off to go to the island from the cottage, the motorboat parked in the cove... All along I had thought that it would be a man, so I concentrated on Jain and Sagar. It never struck me that Gopal Kutty might be in a woman's disguise, until out of the blue, she decided to leave today. And then the answer flashed in my mind and I simply *knew*!'

'You suspected me?' the scientist asked in surprise.

'Only for a while,' Fulki assured him.

'It was obvious that someone from the cottage was involved. If it was none of the men, then only one person remained. Fernando!' Tina concluded. 'And everything really fell into place when Sagar*ji* reported that his papers were stolen right under our noses. There was only one person in the house who had access to them, apart from all of us. And her sudden decision to leave really clinched the matter.'

Mr Sagar smiled at them all. 'You children are quite spunky and really deserve an award for your alertness and sense of responsibility. You have no idea what a great service you have done to our government. The project I am working on is very useful to the country, but if it falls into the wrong hands, it could prove to be very dangerous. I am working on some new security systems around the border, which will guarantee full protection from the enemies. These two men were working on behalf of some foreign powers but thanks to you spunky cousins, they did not succeed.'

'We are glad we could be of help.' Samir smiled.

Sagar*ji* stretched. 'You know what I'm going to do now? I'm going to take a long nap and then begin work. I've already lost a lot of time, but I need some respite from all this excitement.'

He headed up the stairs to his room.

'What should we do now? After all the excitement, life is going to be quite dull.' Paras sighed. 'I think I'll read for a while.' He fetched the ladder and climbed up to take a look at the top row of books.

'And I have to do something very important,' Fulki spoke up in such a grave voice that everyone looked at her, including Vijju and Ruffy.

From one of her pockets, she extracted the crystal and from the other pocket, she extracted the box. Holding the crystal reverently in her hand, she did *namaskar* to it, as the others watched in surprise. Then she opened the box and carefully placed the crystal on the purple velvet, shut the lid and locked it up.

'What are you doing?' Tina asked, curiously.

'I am locking the crystal away. I've realised that I'm still too young to take it up very seriously. Do you remember last night, before we went into the tunnel, I took the crystal in my palm? I was praying that the boys would be safe and hoping to feel the answer in the crystal. But I did not *feel* or *see anything*! I knew then, what the crystal was trying to tell me. I was beginning to depend too much on it. I needed to depend on my instinct and seek the answers and the courage inside me. And that's what I did and that's what I am going to do from now on. So, I am keeping the crystal away and shall use it only when I grow up.'

The others stared at her. Samir ruffled up her curls and grinned.

'I do believe you are growing up, little sis,' he said and Fulki looked pleased.

'Good thought, Fulki,' Paras called down from where he was perched on the ladder.

Tina hugged her cousin.

Footsteps clattered down the stairs and Sagar's voice boomed, 'Panna! Who's been to my room? Where are my....'

'Not again!' the children groaned.

Sagar looked at them and suddenly grinned. 'My glasses? I've come searching for my glasses,' he explained.

'You left them on the table,' Panna called from the kitchen.

'Thanks.' He vanished into the other room.

'Whew! For a moment my heart fluttered in anxiety.' Samir laughed.

'Not only did my heart flutter, my glasses also shook and are right now at the bottom of the ladder,' Paras called with a wide grin. 'Please hand them to me, somebody.'

'Come on down, bookworm. And let's go out. It's a wonderful, sunny day,' Fulki said, threatening to shake the ladder.

Paras laughed. 'Okay, okay, I'm coming down.'

'Yes, let's go to the beach.' Vijju stood up.

Ruffy barked his agreement, prancing joyfully. The spunky cousins set off down the hill, plucking mangoes on the way from the garden, feeling happy and on the top of the world as they headed toward the sunny, golden beach.

Zara laughed. "Okay, okay. I'm coming down!"

"Yes, let's go to the beach," Vijay stood up.

Rusty barked his agreement, prancing joyfully. The spunky cousins set off down the hill, plucking mangoes on the way from the garden, feeling happy and on the top of the world as they headed toward the sunny, golden beach.

Acknowledgements

I am really thrilled to present my 15th book but the first children's novel in the series—The Spunky Cousins.

Mystery at Malabar Cottage is the culmination of my first-ever dream—my dream to be an author who created worlds of entertaining mysteries for children. Growing up on a feast of Enid Blyton books, I wanted to create fictitious worlds of fun and mystery for children and live on in their memories in the form of stories and characters and so here I begin....

A huge thanks to my 'rockstar' agent Suhail Mathur of The Book Bakers for finding the perfect home for this novel.

My deep gratitude to the dynamic Dipankar Mukherjee and Readomania for taking up this series with an infectious and inspiring enthusiasm.

A heartfelt thank you to Rima Kar Ghosh and Indrani Ganguly for meticulously editing the novel and Mistunee Chowdhury for the amazing illustrations. Working with the Readomania team is always such a pleasure!

Immense gratitude to all my readers, who keep my faith in writing alive and especially now to all those children who will fulfill my dream of being THEIR author.

A huge thank you to my family for supporting me in my journey and being a patient and encouraging part of my life.

And finally, a heartfelt thank you to the Universe and God…I feel blessed and grateful every step of the creative way….

Dr Manjiri Prabhu

Pune, July 2019

About the Author

Dr Manjiri Prabhu holds a Doctorate in Communication Science and is an independent filmmaker for Television, an award-winning international Writer/Novelist and also the Founder/Director of two Festivals. She has directed over 200 children's TV programmes, more than 50 short fiction and travel films and has authored 14 books.

Her unpublished psychological thriller novel was adapted into a Hindi feature film by NFDC, titled *Kuchh Dil Ne Kaha*. Her thesis, converted into a book, titled *Roles: Reel and Real*, has become a rare reference book for students of Hindi cinema. Prabhu has been acknowledged as a pioneer in India among women writers of mystery fiction, and she has a diverse global fan following. She is also the first female mystery author to be published outside India and has been labelled as the *'Desi Agatha Christie'*. And much recently, Prabhu has been acknowledged to be a 'match for Dan Brown' by Dr Shashi Tharoor. She has been invited to reputed International Literature Festivals like the Agatha Christie Festival, UK and International Women Fiction Writers, Matera, Italy.

Her novels—*The Cosmic Clues* was selected as a Killer Book by Independent Mystery Booksellers of America and *The Astral Alibi* was honoured as a Notable Book in the Kiriyama Prize. Her books have been published by varied reputed publishers like Penguin, Bloomsbury, Random House USA, Jaico Books, Rupa Publications, Readomania and Times Group Books.

As the Founder/Director of Pune International Literary Festival, Prabhu has placed Pune city on the international map of literature and arts festivals. She believes that literature heals and is a prerequisite to a peaceful society. Recently, she also founded the International Festival of Spiritual India (For Humanities and Spiritual Wisdom).

She has recently been awarded the *Inspirational Women of Maharashtra—Excellence in the field of Writing* (2017) and *Most Admired Leader of Maharashtra* by ERTC Global Herald (2017). She was also awarded the *Rex Karmaveer Gold*

Medal Award (2016) instituted by iCONGO and the UN.

She is also an animal welfare activist promoting caring and adoption of stray dogs.